torn air

thanks to
Slim and Sue, who read the stories
Westfield 6th, for a certain bottle of
Moet et Chandon and their own inimitable
brand of moral support
Olga Norris and the gang at Abelard
who made it all possible
special thanks to
Rose, Jenny, Joy, Andy W, Craig, Katy,
Sime, Judy, Phil D, Anne, Susan, Jenny, JJ,
(Joe) Nick, Gina, Karen and everyone else who's
kept me reasonably sane since I started writing.
I owe you

torn air

david hutchinson

abelard

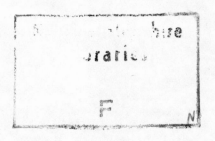

British Library Cataloguing in Publication Data
Hutchinson, David
Torn air.
I. Title
823'.9'1FS   PR6058.U82

ISBN 0-200-72691-9

Abelard-Schuman Limited
A Member of the Blackie Group
Furnival House, 14/18 High Holborn
London WC1V 6BX

Printed in Great Britain by
The Anchor Press Ltd
Tiptree, Essex

contents

It is here, Hamlet. Hamlet, thou art slain;
No med'cine in the world can do thee good.
In thee there is not half an hour's life.
The trecherous Instrument is in thy hand,
Unbated and envenomed. The foul Practice
Hath turned itself on me.

Hamlet, V. ii.

sleepy eyes

It was seeing the gamekeeper that morning that first got George onto the subject of poaching. We were taking a break from cleaning Mrs Brooks's windows, and sitting on the front step having tea and sandwiches, when the keeper came past the house. I'd been in the village long enough to know him by sight, so I didn't take much notice.

George, however, tugged a forelock and called, "Mornin', Mr Murdstone."

Murdstone gave us the eye as he went past, but he didn't stop or offer a reply. His face looked as if it had been carved from a glacier. On his heels was a huge great Dobermann that must have been three feet tall at the shoulder. It was black as sin, and he called it Spot.

"Now there goes a very clever man," said George, watching the keeper walk away.

"How so, George?"

"Very clever keeper, Bertie Murdstone. Used to poach 'imself, so they say. Up near Aviemore." He prononunced it 'Ayvymoor'.

"It's pronounced Aviemore," I said, my patriotic feeling slightly hurt.

George nodded slowly. "Aye, you'd know about that. They always say as 'ow the best keepers are reformed poachers." He bit

7

into one of Mrs Brooks's spam sandwiches. "And 'e's the best."

I took a swig from George's tea tin. "If I were Lord Western I wouldn't trust an ex-poacher to be my gamekeeper," I said. "Besides, you were being very polite to him, weren't you?"

"Aye, I was. I've a great respect for yon keeper. Many's the time 'e's nabbed me rabbiting in them there woods."

I smiled. "You don't poach do you, George?"

"I do that," he said. "Now and again, anyhow."

"Just now and again, George?"

He grinned, and I could see the scatter of burst capillaries on either side of his squashed boxer's nose. He'd never done any boxing that he'd told me about. His old lady had once chucked the frying pan at him, and George had been too full of best bitter to duck.

"Thing is," George went on, "Bertie Murdstone yonder always turns out that bit smarter than I am."

I knew George better than that. "Always?"

"Well, sometimes. He's been bloody close more'n once, though."

We went back to cleaning the windows, and as we finished them before dinnertime George proposed doing another house. As it turned out, we finished two more houses before packing in for the day, so we had extra beer money for that evening.

I think it was the bitter that brought the subject back that evening. George always tended to get a little vociferous as he filled up, and as we leaned on the bar in the Black Bull the conversation steered somehow back onto poaching.

"Poachin's been in my family for years, you know," he said.

"Bunch of crooks, the lot of you," I said.

"S'not like thievin', you know," he defended. "It's an art. 'Sides, sometimes it were the only way we'd 'ave fresh meat."

I sipped my pint and remembered my father telling me something similar one damp and misty morning as he taught me to tickle trout in the chill mountain burns.

George pouted. "My ol' dad used to be able to hypnotise rabbits."

"What?"

He looked rather hurt, as if he'd let go of some great long-guarded secret. "Nowt," he mumbled. " 'Ere, I'll buy you another one."

Walking home down the cool, silent lanes, I said, "Hypnotise rabbits?"

George had used all his extra beer money and was trying to pick up the shadows of the trees in the moonlight. "They used to say as 'ow my ol' dad could charm the little buggers up out of their 'oles."

I shook my head. "I don't believe it."

He gave a disgusted little snort and fell over. "You townies are all t'same," he said as I helped him up.

"I'm not a townie," I said.

"Think there's a machine as puts the yellow stuff into eggs," he rumbled on.

"I'm not a townie," I said again.

"Think as 'ow there's one tit on a cow for t'cream an' all."

"George," I said. "I'm not a townie."

"Ah, bugger it," he mumbled, and we walked the rest of the way in silence.

"Hypnotise rabbits?" I said the next morning.

"Just 'old the ladder, Paul."

"I'm intrigued now, George. How did your old man hypnotise rabbits?"

"Ah, that'd be tellin'." He came back down the ladder to fill his bucket with clean water. He was a big oaken door of a man in his middle forties, but for all his size he moved carefully, gracefully, as if he'd once had dancing lessons.

"Well you can at least clue me in about it, can't you?"

Wringing out his chamois leather, he shook his head.

"I'll wait until you're at the top of the ladder, and then I'll take it away," I said.

He straightened up and looked at me. "Do you really want to know?"

"Yes."

His face had the look of a man fed up with being bothered. "Let's 'ave a tea break then," he suggested.

9

George's father had been the best poacher in the county, according to George. He had died, aged eighty-five, trying to get out of a wood with a sack full of pheasants over his shoulder. For as long as George could remember, the old man had always gone out of a Wednesday night and come back hours later with two or three rabbits for them to hang in the outhouse. Later, he'd taught George how to do it.

I said, "It's a nice idea, George, but you can't hypnotise a rabbit."

He smiled. "Now, my ol' mum used to say that to my dad. 'Eric,' she'd say, 'rabbits en't got no brains as you can hypnosymitise.' But we always 'ad rabbit when we wanted rabbit."

"And your dad taught you how to do it?"

"He did. Nowt to it." And I could see an odd gleam in his eye. I could almost see the great crafty machinery turning in his head. "Show you tonight."

I thought, this I have to see. Fatal mistake.

It was a lovely night, with just a sliver of moon in a dark blue velvet sky. Akin's Wood was a raggedy silhouette with a fluffy top against the sky. I'd put on black cord trousers and a black turtle-neck sweater. George had on an ex-army camouflage jacket and carried a black nylon rucksack. We didn't say a thing to each other as we made our way slowly up the hill towards the wood.

Everything was quiet in the wood, but strange unseen things made hooting noises, or snuffled about in the leaf clutter. I wasn't used to being in woodland.

We stopped in a little clearing. George sat me down in a great hollow-hearted patch of dead fern and briar where I couldn't be seen, and told me to stay silent no matter what happened. He found another patch of fern and lay down on his stomach, half in, half out of it, and didn't move again.

I sighed and tried to make myself comfortable. It looked like being a long cold night.

I lost track of time, and almost dozed off. The moon rose and began to set, and George hadn't moved a muscle. It seemed a ridiculous way of poaching. The unseen things still shuffled about among the trees, and I wished I'd brought a coat as well.

Around two in the morning, something came softly crackling through the undergrowth, and I awoke with a start. I could see everything quite clearly. A movement in the undergrowth caught the corner of my eye, and I followed it slowly, quite awake now. The rabbit hopped out into the moonlight-dappled clearing. George still didn't move.

The rabbit, a big brown one, hopped slowly across the clearing, taking its time in the moonlight. George lay motionless, as he had done for the past hour, and the rabbit hopped past him so close he could have grabbed it, but he didn't move, didn't even seem to be breathing. The rabbit looked at me, and stopped, and I waited for it to startle and run away, but it didn't. It didn't do anything; it just sat there transfixed, and I suddenly realised it wasn't looking at me at all. It was looking at George.

My stomach tingled. George had hypnotised the rabbit.

Still George lay unmoving, and ten minutes later another rabbit came out of the ferns. It went over to the transfixed one, sniffed curiously at it, looked about, saw George, and was suddenly nailed to the spot. I took a long slow breath. It was all getting a little eerie.

In the moonlight, another rabbit hopped out to meet its fate. And another. And another.

George had eight rabbits standing before him when something larger pushed its way through the undergrowth, and a large vixen stepped out into the clearing. The place must have looked like paradise to her. The rabbits stayed where they were, and I held my breath as the vixen, brush held high, stepped jauntily across the clearing to them. George could, I reasoned, afford to lose at least one.

The vixen bent her head, mouth open, and stopped. Frozen. I blinked.

Another fox came into the clearing, walked up to its mate, sniffed cautiously, and looked at George.

And stayed looking at George.

It was too much. "That's enough, George," I whispered. We'd been there about three hours.

Something else came through the undergrowth. Something big. I saw the gun before he stepped into the clearing, and I sank back into the shadows of the bushes.

"George, it's the keeper!" I hissed.

The keeper came through the briars and stopped when he saw George and the animals. The great black Dobermann was at his heels. He lifted the gun and said, "All right, stand up."

George lifted his head, then got up stiffly, and there was something funny about the way Murdstone's gun didn't follow him. It was only when George stepped to one side and the keeper didn't move that I realised he'd hypnotised Murdstone as well.

George stooped and patted the dog. It didn't move. He turned and grinned at me, and I sat there for one dreadful moment, waiting to be mesmerised, but nothing happened. I smiled weakly, just because I was still in full possession of my senses. I stood up and walked over to him.

" 'Ow about that?" he said innocently.

I stepped up to Murdstone, tapped him hesitantly on the shoulder, but he didn't move. "This is silly."

"Nothin's silly if it works," George said with bluff philosophy.

"How do you do it?"

He grinned. "That'd be tellin'."

"Don't play about, George."

He shook his head. "My ol' dad told me, 'Tha's got to know 'ow to use it, Georgie'."

I knew I couldn't talk him round this time, so I shrugged and waved my hand in front of Murdstone's eyes, but he didn't even blink. His eyes looked odd; the pupils were dilated until there was only a thin rind of white on them. The dog's eyes were the same.

"Very impressive," I said. "Now wake them up."

George was going about popping rabbits into the rucksack. It was as easy as picking up beanbags. He stopped and looked at me. "You're kidding."

"I am not."

He straightened up, thrust the rabbit he had been holding into the rucksack, and stepped over to me. "Poaching is against the law, Paul," he said, very slowly, enunciating every syllable, just so I'd understand.

"I don't care," I said. "We can't leave him here."

George smiled his big slow smile. The moonlight made it look demonic. "Well I dunno . . ."

"Wake him up, George," I said.

He put the rucksack down and scratched his head. "Well now," he said, "I never 'ad to wake nothing up afore."

I suddenly felt cold. "You don't know how to," I said.

"Now, Paul, I didn't say that."

"But that's what you meant, isn't it?" I looked at that huge motionless Dobermann and shuddered.

George shrugged. "Never needed to wake 'em up afore. Just knock 'em on t'ead and put 'em in t'pot."

"We can't knock him on the head and put him in the pot, George." He grinned, and I said, "George."

"Never crossed me mind," he said, but he didn't stop smiling.

"Come on, George. Wake him up."

He shrugged. "Don't know 'ow."

I closed my eyes. "Oh God, George, this is kidnapping."

"Nay! We en't taken 'im nowhere!"

"Be serious, George. You can't just . . . hypnotise people like that."

George looked bemused. "Weren't my fault. 'E just got in t'way."

I was starting to panic now. Murdstone and his dog looked like waxworks, only they were breathing.

"George, come on, think. Didn't your dad ever say anything about waking them up?"

He shook his head. " 'E never 'ad to wake 'em up neither."

"George!" I hissed. "He could stay like that!"

He acknowledged the possibility with a nod and a slight smile, and my mind started to trip through all the hypnotist acts I'd ever seen or heard of. I had this horrible cold desperate feeling in the pit of my stomach. I should have taken to my heels then and there.

"Mr Murdstone," I said desperately, "when I count to three and snap my fingers I want you to wake up. One two three."

Snap.

Nothing.

"Mr Murdstone, I want you to nod if you understand me."

Murdstone's head moved slightly. I jumped back about a yard, but he didn't move again, and the dog didn't seem about to rip my throat out. I was shaking when I stepped in front of him once more and looked into those great empty eyes.

"Mr Murdstone. Give me the gun."

Murdstone finally straightened up from the half-crouch he had been frozen into, eyes still staring straight ahead, and held the gun out in both hands. I took it from him gently, broke it, took out the cartridges and pocketed them, closed the gun, and put the thing back in his hands. The fingers curled about it automatically.

George had gone back to bagging the rabbits. I watched him manhandle the vixen into the rucksack, then its mate. He did the rucksack up and put it over one shoulder, looked at me, and raised an eyebrow. And I suddenly realised that to George this was an important victory over the keeper. I wondered if perhaps George hadn't known that Murdstone would come through the undergrowth tonight, wondered if perhaps it hadn't all been one big set up, just to make the keeper look stupid. Too bad. I had an idea now.

"We can leave him at the side of a road," I said, which seemed to suit George.

I could get the keeper to walk, but the dog wouldn't budge.

"Mean bugger, even when it's awake," George said sagely. He smiled again, and I got the impression that he was terribly amused by the whole thing.

We must have looked ridiculous; George with the rucksack full of mesmerised rabbits and foxes, Murdstone walking like something from a bad horror movie, and me with Murdstone's dog across my shoulders. Only it wasn't funny.

We were almost out of the woods, literally as well as figuratively, when something rustled and yawned in front of us. I quietly ordered Murdstone to stop and stood his dog up beside him and went to confer with George. My shoulders ached.

" 'E must've brought Billy Freeman with him," George whispered. "Billy won't be pleased about bein' taken' away from 'is missus at this time o' night."

"If you can't say anything constructive don't say anything at all," I said. "Where'll he be?"

" 'E'll be down by t'gate onto t'main road, waitin' for us to come out." Those great warm eyes regarded me without concern, waiting for me to think of something.

"Can't we go round, through the trees?"

George nodded. "Aye, we could. But we'd make an 'ell of a row."

"I think you're enjoying this," I said. And I had an idea.

I still couldn't get the dog to move. I said, "Mr Murdstone, tell your dog to heel."

Murdstone snapped his fingers, and from that moment the Dobermann was on his heels. I handed Murdstone the rucksack, spoke quietly to him, then stepped out into the open. If we were lucky, everything would happen right.

Billy Freeman jumped down off the fence and stubbed out his fag as we approached the gate, and I knew Murdstone and that great black dog were right behind me, and I kept right on walking. It was all going to be okay.

I was level with Freeman when I felt this great hard cruel hand on my shoulder, and a soft voice behind me said, "Nearly made it this time, George."

I looked at George, and George looked at me. "You 'ad to try to wake 'im up didn't you, you clever bugger," he said.

thumbprints

I got lost twice driving to Coombe Bassett. Not that I've ever been the best navigator, but the village was so small it only appeared on my OS map of the Chilterns anyway, and the roads were starting to deteriorate and roadsigns had been removed by conservationists or museums or vandals. A gliding club was using part of the A41 near Hemel Hempstead as a runway and I had to go round them, which was why I wound up lost the first time.

I ran out of petrol near Aylesbury and topped up at what must have been the only filling station left operating in Buckinghamshire. I got a set of reliable local directions, and twenty minutes later I was lost again, motoring down narrow side roads which were being claimed by the overgrowing hedges on either side. Twice I had to stop and move fallen trees out of the way. It broke my heart to see the roads going like this, but I supposed it was better than seeing them get torn up by great impersonal machines.

I only found my way to Pagden House by stopping every time I saw a human being and asking the way. As a result of all this I was three hours overdue and everyone was worrying about me.

"We were worrying about you," said Eakins when I showed up at the door with my suitcase.

"Lying sod," said Len Bister. "Where's Jim?"

"Give up," I said.

"He isn't here yet," said Bister. "We thought you were driving him down."

I stepped through the doorway. "Can I come in?"

Eakins came back to life. "Er, yes. Your bedroom's on the second floor. Tom can show you where it is after you've had dinner."

"I want to see the gear first."

Bister made a disgusted sound. "Can't think of anything but work."

Eakins said, "Have a rest first, Neil. There's no hurry."

I put my case down and walked across the hall. "And it better all be here too," I said to nobody in particular.

The dining room had once been richly furnished, with a great long dining table and lots of high-backed chairs and chandeliers, paintings on the walls and all that. After a great deal of pleading and promising, the National Trust had been persuaded to remove the furniture and put it in store, leaving the empty room to our tender ministrations. The room was now an unholy clutter of electronic instruments and equipment. A knitting-bag of cables, some as thick as my thumb, spilled across the floor, some of them taped down to stop people falling over them, others not. Six oscillograph cabinets stood along one wall, and a little IBM 6200359 in one corner with a kettle on it because the only spare socket was in that corner. Ranks of detectors, recorders, video cameras all over the place. We were going to play merry hell with Pagden House's electricity bill.

Just off-centre in the room stood a tall wire-mesh box, about half again as tall as a tall man; it reached to about three feet below the ceiling, the very fine mesh stretched over a strong frame. It was scrupulously grounded, but I didn't bother to check now. We could do that later. The whole mess looked horribly out of place with the rich panelling and painted ceiling and polished oak floor, but everything was there that should have been there, so I decided to let it go and started thinking about food and where the hell Singh had got to.

Singh came walking up the long conifer-lined drive around six with a suitcase in one hand, a plastic carrier bag in the other, and a rucksack over one shoulder. He looked like he was ready for a fortnight at Butlin's. Typical Singh. He'd used the gate and reached the village in nothing halved.

"You lazy sod," I said as I opened the door. He'd sold his car years ago, before transplacement made it worth next to nothing.

"I bet I've done more walking today than you have," he said tiredly. The house was about a mile from the gate in the village.

"I walked four miles to find a petrol station this morning," I said.

He stepped into the hall. "Serves you right for not topping up before you left."

"It might have been easier if we hadn't made filling stations extinct."

"I like the 'we'."

I shrugged. If anything ever went wrong with a gate, it was always my fault, and it was usually me who people complained to. Not Singh; not NASA, to whom we'd taken transplacement first on the premise that it was instant space travel, and who had done all the development before finding out it wasn't. None of them. Me, the man who'd had his picture in all the papers. Singh said it was the price of fame. Every car manufacturer in the world hated me. Still, the roads were a lot quieter now . . .

"I don't know what you're complaining about," I said. "You're the one who uses the things."

Singh nodded thoughtfully. "True," he assented. "Is everything okay?"

"Everything's here, if that's what you mean. All ready to go."

Singh nodded again. "Okay. We'll do a rundown tomorrow before we turn it on. Now then, where's the tucker?"

I grinned and chalked up a small victory. Even using instantaneous travel, Singh had managed to miss dinner.

We ate breakfast downstairs in the kitchen the next morning. It was a big cool room, dominated by a big food preparation table, its top scarred by generations of cooks chopping meat on it, and a smaller dining table. The floor was freshly scrubbed flags. Back in the days of the Sixth Earl, the servants would have eaten down here. The house's caretaker, Willis, lived in what had once been part of the servants' quarters, adjoining the kitchen. He ate breakfast with us and didn't seem overly worried about what we were up to. I could hardly blame him. He was getting paid, after all. He seemed rather fascinated by the theory behind it all. Being us, we indulged him.

"So when someone dies," Eakins finished, "he leaves behind this discontinuity in the rate of entropy, and the aura around his body which caused the discontinuity in the first place remains for a little while before draining away. Now do you see?"

Willis scratched his head and looked at all the diagrams we'd scribbled for him. He was thirtyish, clean-shaven and casually dressed. He smiled slightly. "Sorry, fellers, but a Second in Classical Architecture doesn't really equip you for all this jazz."

Eakins sighed.

Willis said, "This energy field. The aura. It surrounds all living things, right? I've seen some Kirlian pictures, so don't think I don't believe you and all, but it's hard to accept that ghosts are just fading fields of energy . . ."

Colin Cook shrugged. "It's like an after-image. A sort of negative left behind in the entropic eddy the organism maintained while it was alive. Nothing heavy."

"Yeah," said Willis, "but if that's true, then everything that was ever alive leaves an eddy behind it when it dies. All the trees and the insects and animals—"

"That's right," said Singh, stirring his spoon about in dry cornflakes, "but the dents they make in entropy aren't very radical, and the energy dissipates in a very short time. Seconds sometimes. It all depends on the strength of the aura."

Tom Watt nodded. We were better than a music-hall act once we got talking shop. "That's why you tend to get murdered people or people who died violently coming back as ghosts. If a lot of energy's associated with the death the eddy persists longer. Takes more energy to kill a man than you'd realise."

20

"And sometimes you get events associated with energy persisting as well," said Singh. "Things like old battles or bad train crashes. We reckon there's a huge eddy over Hiroshima and Nagasaki. A sort of negative image of the original explosions."

Willis pursed his lips. "That's wild," he said. "Persistence of vision on a cosmic scale."

Len Bister put back his head and laughed, and I smiled and tucked into my cornflakes, while Eakins went into Act Two.

"We think that if the eddy is supplied with energy, it won't drain away, but deepen and gain strength, and so will the energy field within it."

"And that's what you're going to try to do?" said Willis.

Singh nodded. "We're going to capture a ghost and pump it with energy and see what happens."

A year before, something similar had happened in Wiltshire, with a pattern of three transplacement gates tapping energy from the Earth's magnetic field through the old ley line system. The transplacement fields had attracted loose entropic eddies and they had somehow fed on the energy. It had been fascinating then, in a scary sort of way, but I wanted to try it for myself under controlled conditions. And here in Pagden House the conditions were perfect. Pagden House was haunted.

After breakfast we moved into the dining room and started to turn on the equipment. We set about tuning the oscilloscopes, running programs through the computer and checking the Faraday Cage's grounding and setting the trap. Willis must have thought we were all just a little mad. We might have been too.

The door of the cage was fitted with four very strong springs, and it locked back at about a hundred degrees from closed. On the floor inside the cage were dozens of scrawled notations in felt pen which would wash off later; measurements and lines and things, and a big X of yellow Sellotape. Probes and things hung down a short distance from the roof of the cage, connected to the detectors by cables.

Singh fetched the carrier bag he had brought with him the day before, and took out a black plastic box about the same size as a shoebox. There was an on/off switch in one end and a connection for a cable in the other. It was heavy; you could tell that by the way he handled it. He gave it to Colin, who took it over to the cage.

"This is what it's all about," Singh explained to Willis. "It's a transplacement generator. That cross on the floor marks the spot where three ley lines cross. We put the generator on the spot, align it properly, and when we turn it on the field will start tapping the Earth's magnetic field through the ley lines. If all this activity does attract a ghost, the detectors will register the change in energy levels and spring the door. Being a field of energy, it won't be able to pass the grounded walls of the cage, so it'll be stuck there while the generator pumps it with energy."

"And you really expect to catch a ghost?" said Willis.

"No," said Len, "we like spending long weekends like this." Bister and Willis didn't much like each other.

"Len," said Eakins from the computer terminal. "Somebody thinks we'll succeed, Mr Willis. We're being paid to do this."

"All hail to our benefactors," Colin said, kneeling in the cage and connecting the generator to a cable which came through the mesh wall. He put it down on the tape cross, adjusted it until the cross matched marks on the box, then backed out.

Everybody looked at me. I bent over a panel of switches, turned on the detectors, then nodded at Colin, who turned the generator on at the socket. The door clicked free and whipped shut with a loud crack and was automatically locked.

"Well at least everything works," said Len.

Willis looked at Singh for an explanation. Singh said, "The generator's tapping the Earth's magnetic field now; that's what set the door off. What we do now is calibrate the detectors so the generator doesn't set them off, but any alien energy fields will."

Willis frowned. "Won't the generator . . . um . . . transmit all the air in the room to wherever transmitted things go?"

"It isn't turned up high enough for that," said Tom. "Just idling over."

"What are you going to do once you've got it all sorted out?"

"Sit down and wait," said Eakins.

Recalibration took us about an hour. We turned on the generator, made sure the trap was properly set, and left it.

Singh had this theory, stemming from the work he'd done when we'd first found Preston's notes on transplacement. It was first cousin to something called Kramer's Footprint Theory, which was basically what we'd been trying to tell Willis that morning. All living things have an aura, and this, being an energy field, upsets the rate at which the energy of the Universe is gradually draining away, causing a discontinuity. A 'dent' in entropy. If you assume certain things, Kramer's theory explains ghosts and all sorts of joyful parapsychological phenomena.

Singh's theory was that the Galaxy, and probably the entire Universe, was a ghost-image of something else, and that entropy was the gradual fading-away of the image. "A great big smudged thumb-print fading on the face of Creation," was the way he liked to put it. The upshot of all this, he contended, was that when entropy reaches its maximum, many billions of years from now, everything will simply . . . fade away.

I'm naturally distrustful of metaphysics. I'm real; I bleed if I cut myself shaving; I get drunk if I have enough ale. I'm not an energy field chasing around in an entropic eddy; I'm full of atoms and particles and cells and things. Corporeal, which Singh's model of the Universe is not.

However, now and again I get to thinking, How do you know? You judge reality by your surroundings, and if the whole Universe is a ghost, how are you going to know if you're real or not?

I don't really care, but Singh did. He cared a lot, and he'd been the one who had done most of the organisation for the experiment at Pagden House. Ghosts were undergoing the same entropic process as the Universe, and Singh wanted to talk to them, to ask them if his theory was right. He had to know whether the Universe was real or not. Personally, I didn't think we'd be able to communicate with any ghost we caught. Blind instinct printed on thin air. That was all they were, by their very nature. All I wanted to do was see what happened if you energised a ghost. Just being able to call them was enough.

We waited, and for a while nothing happened.

Two days after we turned on the generator I was coming downstairs to breakfast when I found Bister on the phone. He was staring puzzledly at the handset and tapping the cradle and muttering to himself.

"What's up, Len?" I asked, stopping on my way to the steps down to the kitchen.

"Phone's shot," he said, pursing his lips and tapping the cradle again.

I walked over, took the handset and listened. There was nothing but static on the other end. Lines were falling into disrepair nowadays, I knew, but I'd never heard anything like this. Tapping the cradle momentarily broke up the static, but didn't stop it. "There's a phone at the end of the drive," I said. "I'll phone the engineers after breakfast."

In the kitchen, the transistor radio was spitting and crackling like a basketful of wildcats. Eakins and Colin Cook sat looking at it, sipping their tea.

"Phone's out," I said, pouring myself a bowl of cornflakes and sitting down.

Eakins nodded and sipped at his tea. Colin said, "Willis's telly stopped working at twelve last night. Static; all channels."

I looked at the tranny and said, "The generator."

Across the breakfast table, we all looked at each other. Eakins said, "Hm."

The effect didn't stop, but it didn't get any worse either. It didn't seem to be affecting the instruments in the dining room, though, so we took the tranny in there and the static cleared. Finally, something was happening.

Using the tranny and the floorplans we'd used to mark the position of the leys, we mapped out the extent of the dead spot. It turned out to be a fifty-foot circle, with the generator at its centre. We sat and thought about it a lot, but we couldn't make any sense of it. I'd expected static effects, but not starting twenty-five feet from the generator. The effect went down in the experiment notes, together with lots of drawings. Since Willis kept complaining that we'd ruined his telly, we dubbed it the Willis Effect, but that didn't placate him. We wrote it down in the notes to make it legal, but he still grumbled. There's no pleasing some people.

I went down to the village four days after we turned on the generator. Coombe Bassett was indeed a tiny, secluded thing, lost and dreaming in the lush Chiltern forests, its half-timber houses buried in great scented gardens. There was only one shop still in business, a tiny general shop. A hundred yards down the street was a red pillar box, absolutely useless now. Beside it was a tall gateway of dull metal tubes, with a pushbutton dial attached at chest height to one of the uprights. All gates look the same. As I went into the shop someone came out of the gate, looked round, cursed silently, turned, dialled, and was gone again. Wrong number.

Inside, the shop was dark and cosy. It smelled of tea and old wood and packets of toy pistol caps and sherbet and newspapers. In one corner an old fridge hummed and rocked on its springs. In the cool dimness a young woman stood marking newspapers. An old woman stood behind the counter, reading a magazine. She looked up as I entered the shop, and smiled at me. The young woman went on marking the newspapers.

I picked up a wad of newspapers, laid them on the counter. The old woman totted up the prices, and I paid her.

"You're one of the scientists who're working up at the Big House, aren't you?" she said as I bundled up the papers.

It occurred to me that in a village this size a stranger couldn't stay hidden for very long, and that even with the gate, the number of people visiting Coombe Bassett would be tiny at best. "That's right," I said.

She screwed up her eyes behind tortoiseshell-rimmed spectacles. "You're the one who invented the matter transmitters, aren't you?"

I didn't bat an eyelid. You can get used to people recognising you. "I'm Neil Judson," I said.

The young woman looked up for a moment, then went back to

the papers. The old woman said, "You do know there's only this shop left now, since that gate was put in?"

I sighed inwardly. I didn't want an argument. "Yes, I saw," I said.

She didn't seem angry, for some silly reason. "Nobody comes here now. They can just as easily go to London, or America."

I nodded. "So can you," I said. "People have to adapt. We can't forget transplacement now it's here."

There was a time when I'd get threatening letters from car workers and road menders. All the transport workers in the world had a right to dislike me I suppose, but like I said, people have to adapt. Transplacement had changed a lot of things for the better too, though. The cost of living was heading down for the first time in almost ninety years; transporting goods cost almost nothing. In theory, it put an end to slums; people didn't have to live crammed up together any more.

The old woman shook her head. "I wasn't asking for excuses, Mr Judson. I wanted to know if you cared."

"They want to know if I care," I said, tossing the papers down on the kitchen table.

Singh looked up from his notes. "Who do?"

I sat down. "People in the village. They want to know if I care about what transplacement's doing to the world."

He put down his pen and smiled. "Do you?"

I shrugged. "How do you define it? I care that I can't get a gallon of petrol when I want it. I care that things are cheaper. I care that I can't use the A41 near Hemel Hempstead because they're landing gliders on it. Do *you* care?"

He shrugged, and got up and poured us both coffee. "You think too much," he said.

"Thank you," I said.

In the dining room Eakins was playing chess with the computer and Colin Cook was changing the tapes in the video machines. In the hall, Len was wandering about with the tranny and a bit of chalk checking out the dead area. We took turns each morning and evening to check it for any change, but so far it seemed constant. There was a smaller dead circle upstairs, and an even smaller one on the floor above that, each with its centre directly above the generator. The computer extrapolated for us a spherical dead area fifty feet through the centre, with the generator at its heart. Tom Watt had spent two days outside mapping the extent of the active area. This turned out to be another circle, six hundred feet across, and probably part of another sphere. None of us could work out why the configuration was like that, but we kept the generator running anyway. I was beginning to feel like giving up.

Singh was shaking me. I came awake very slowly, dimly aware that Singh was in dressing gown and slippers. "God, Jim, what time is it?"

He kept shaking me. None too gently. "Twenty past two. Are you awake yet?"

I turned over. "No. Shove off."

He shook me again. Harder. "Come on, Neil. We've got a capture."

I was awake all in one go, and running downstairs with half the bedclothes still wrapped around me. I burst into the dining room and came to a stop just past the doorway.

Every 'scope in the room was going mad. The pen traces made peaks that went right off the paper. The door of the cage was shut, but as far as I could see it was empty. Eakins, wearing only his pyjama bottoms and with a fag hanging out of the corner of his mouth, was sitting typing as fast as he could at the computer terminal. Tom and Len were scribbling numbers from the 'scopes and Colin was hopelessly trying to sort out the scrambled piles of paper tape from the pen-recorders. Everyone should have been shouting, but there wasn't a sound save for Eakins swearing every so often at a typing mistake.

Bleary eyes screwed up, I squinted at the oscilloscopes, then at the cage, then back again. No doubt about it. There was some kind of energy field in the cage, and we'd caught the bugger.

"Everything cool?" I asked, which was an idiot question, but I was starting to go back to sleep again.

Eakins didn't look up. He shook his head and went on typing.

"Great," I said, sitting down and pulling the bedclothes around my shoulders. I pulled a tin of beer from a fourpack on the table, and opened it. It was likely to be a long night. Or morning. Or day, come to that.

The energy in the cage levelled off at twenty past five. Through the dining room windows I watched the great pastel orange sun climb up out of the woods and set light to the morning mist. I saw a fox dart across the huge lawn, a chicken in its mouth almost too big for it to carry, and vanish into the bushes far away at the end of the lawn. Dimly above the sound of the IBM printing things out I could hear the dawn chorus calling the sun up from its dark lair. I opened the window to let out the stale mixture of fag-smoke and sweat that we'd been breathing, and a breeze that smelled of huge woods and downlands gusted through the room.

"Shut the window, Neil," Eakins said without stopping typing. "You're making a draught."

Singh was sitting on a stool, staring at the cage, chin on fist, silent.

We took turns logging the data and typing it into the computer for correlation. The sun laboured slowly into the sky, and we turned the lights off as the day gained its own momentum. Willis came in at six, rubbing his hand through his hair and yawning. The sight of five sleep-starved, unshaven, slightly crazed scientists stopped him dead in his carpet slippers.

"Have you got one?" he asked quietly.

"Yeah," Singh breathed.

Willis walked over to the cage, wondering no doubt why we were still all in pyjamas, and peered through the mesh. "Can't see anything."

"It should become visible as it picks up energy," said Colin.

"Oh," he said. "I wonder who it is."

"Maybe it's the Sixth Earl," Len muttered with a small smile.

"Mm," said Singh. "Yeah."

The theory was sound; I knew that. I'd stood at Stonehenge in the middle of a huge thunderstorm and watched ghosts coming through a gate. I knew it should be working and that any moment now the ghost would become visible.

It didn't.

There was no point in asking the computer about it because it wasn't programmed with enough data to give an answer, so all we could do was wait.

Singh nodded sagely at the cage as Willis brought us breakfast. "It needs seeding."

That made sense. "Yeah," I said. "Maybe it's too weak to tap the fields itself."

Eakins frowned. "All right. Suggestions?"

Singh beat me to it. "Shoot some static through it. We've got a Van der Graaf machine somewhere, haven't we?"

"Not too much, though. We could overload it if we rush," I said.

Eakins nodded. "Okay."

Still in pyjamas, we set up the Van der Graaf generator, ran a cable into the cage, and shot a quarter-million-volt spark through whatever we'd caught. The first pulse went to ground through the wall of the cage, but I figured the spark had passed through the eddy we'd caught inside. We waited an hour, then did it again. And again. It might have been slightly silly, but at least we were doing something. Once more, and we decided enough was enough.

"That should make his hair stand up," Eakins commented. We left it.

After the final pulse of electricity the magnetometers indicated that something odd was starting to happen to the magnetic fields in the room. The transplacement generator, instead of just tapping the fields, was starting to realign them about itself as the ghost began to tap the fields. The energy levels inside the cage started to rise again, which looked promising. Red-eyed, we sat around and waited, and all the while I was missing the most important thing. In the end I drifted away to get dressed and have a shave. At one in the afternoon we had a plate of spam sandwiches for dinner.

It took ten hours for the ghost to assimilate enough surface static to become visible. At first it was no more than a slight subliminal flicker of blue light, but it slowly gained strength and intensity, brightening, a flickering blue line bent into the silhouette of a man. It was sitting motionless on the floor next to the generator like an unfinished still from an animated movie, not yet inked in.

Bister took photos of his own so that some people might believe us. Eakins sat staring at the cage, a pile of fag ends and empty beer tins growing about his feet. Singh sat beside him and never took his eyes off the ghost. And now I knew how he felt. I suddenly wanted to talk to it too. None of us said a word.

Eakins broke the silence finally, around three. "It doesn't seem disturbed."

"It's still feeding," Singh said without looking away from the cage.

Tom said, "I don't want to worry anybody, but if that shape's static electricity, shouldn't it be running to ground?"

We all looked at one another, and for the first time I had the awful conviction that we were too deep in this already. The ghost had started to defy the laws of physics. But then, I suppose it always had been.

Exactly twenty-four hours after we'd captured it, the ghost moved. There was a flurry of activity as we trained all the video cameras on the cage to watch the ghost slowly stand and put its hand out to touch the side of the cage. There was a sharp crack and a bright flash that threw shadows across the room, and the ghost jumped back into the centre of the cage.

"Current flow," said Eakins.

"Maybe it's holding its shape by some kind of surface tension along the boundary of the eddy," said Colin.

"And maybe it's using Sellotape," said Len.

The ghost seemed to fade for a moment, then gained strength again and hesitated. By now it wasn't just a silhouette, but a bright blue line enclosing fainter blue detail. I could dimly glimpse the contours of the face, the chest and abdomen. The eyes were two bright sapphire sparks, cold and inhuman. Every time I looked at it, it seemed to turn those terrible eyes on me. As if it knew me . . .

Without warning it jumped again, flinging its whole body against the mesh. There was another huge discharge, and it fell back, flickering like an electric bulb about to go out. This time it didn't take so long for it to build up strength and decide to try again. This time the discharge almost blinded us all. The instruments went crazy. The cage rocked.

"It's trying to get out," Colin said unnecessarily.

"It won't," Eakins said very calmly; the sort of calm you get from someone who is trying very hard not to panic. "We had the cage built as strong as possible."

And I had that feeling again that we should quit while we were ahead. The ghost wasn't just feeding now. It was sucking up and assimilating energy as fast as it could, and somehow it got stronger every time it tried to get out.

Singh said, "We should be trying to communicate."

Despite events, we all looked at him. "You have to be kidding," said Tom.

I looked at the ghost again, crackling and flickering, and again I wanted to talk to it and discuss the reality of the Universe, but all it did was throw itself against the wall of the cage again and again, building up huge discharges. We'd been right all along. Intelligence died with the body. The aura wasn't intelligent. Pure, blind instinct. Mindless.

Eakins frowned. "We ought to let it go," he mused.

Singh's head jerked round. "No!" he snapped.

"Man, it's *angry*," Colin breathed.

Len, who had gone out for coffee, came back with the transistor radio. It was turned right up and spitting great corruscating peals of static. Somewhere back in my mind it struck me that Len was inside the dead area, but it didn't register. He held the radio out in front of him like an ancient occult charm, and ten feet from the cage the static cleared. He stopped, took a step back, and the static erupted again.

"The dead area's collapsing," he said. "Don't know when it started."

Eakins looked at me, then walked round the cage to the socket the generator was plugged into, and turned it off.

Nothing happened.

Tom rushed out of the door. The main circuit breakers were downstairs, on the wall of the kitchen. A minute later all the lights in the house went out. Still the ghost, a sapphire demon dancing in the sudden dark, flung itself again and again at the cage. Every time it hit the cage wall, the cage jumped up about an inch then crashed back.

Eakins looked sidelong at me, his face lit flickering blue. "The reaction's sustaining itself."

"Damnation!" Bister dropped the radio and dashed out, almost colliding with Tom in the doorway. I heard the front door slam as he took off down the drive to the phone at the bottom. If the dead area was collapsing, the active area might be expanding to put out the phone box. I turned to look out of the window, and saw it was raining outside. Lightning flickered, thunder rumbled, and we'd been too engrossed to notice. And I saw what I'd been missing all this time, what I'd missed at Stonehenge.

The transplacement fields didn't attract the ghosts. They produced lightning! And lightning was energy! Huge, vast amounts of static electricity. That was what attracted the ghosts. And they fed until they could control the storm . . .

Amid all the chaos, I heard a tiny splintering sound from the cage. I turned from the window. Inside the cage, the little black box was shattering all by itself. A spiderweb of cracks had appeared in the top, and smaller ones were agonisingly spreading on the sides. It was as if something was slowly sucking the box in on itself.

Singh looked as if he was having a war with his conscience. I was still buzzing with my revelation. If the ghosts got strong enough to control the lightning, they'd do the logical, instinctive thing . . .

I was already jumping for the cage when Singh yelled, "Do something!"

The clamps, impossible to open from inside the cage, flew open under my fingers. The door flung itself open (it had taken four of us to hold that thing against its springs!) and the blaze of light darted forward.

My head came up. I couldn't get out of the way in time. The ghost rushed towards me, and the blinding outline passed round me

and was gone.

With a sound like a rifle going off, the box imploded. Suddenly a hurricane roared in the room. Sheets of printout whipped into the air and pasted themselves to the walls of the cage. Somewhere, lots of glass shattered. I flung myself at the box, but I couldn't find the switch. The box seemed horribly heavy, as if glued to the floor. I had to get it off the junction of the leys which were powering it. I found the cable, got hold of it, wrenched hard, and felt the generator move under my weight.

The roaring seemed to persist forever, then it weakened, died slowly.

Outside, the thunder started to fade.

It was almost mid-day when I came down to breakfast. Eakins was sitting in the dining room looking at the ruins of our experiment. The hundred-year-old windows had blown in and there was glass everywhere. Someone, I thought, had better think up a good excuse for when the National Trust starts to ask where their windows went.

"Come back to the scene of the crime, eh?" I said.

He took a long drag on his cigarette, exhaled slowly, and looked round. "How do you feel?"

"I'll live. You?"

He shrugged.

"Did we record last night?"

He nodded at the pile of videotape cassettes. "Up to when Tom turned all the power off."

"Missed the best bit then," I said.

He shuddered a little. "Not that anyone's going to believe us." He took out a battered packet of Royals, lit one from the stub of the other. "You don't smoke, do you?" he said.

"That's a nasty rumour," I said. Right now I needed a smoke. I took one and borrowed his lighter. It was the first I'd had since school and it made me cough, but I didn't care any more, because I'd learned a great truth. Cool is good for you. Besides, I had the Judson–Sanderson Effect sussed out now.

"Do you realise," I said, sitting down on the floor, "that it isn't the transplacement fields that attract the ghosts, but the build up of electrostatic energy caused by the magnetic eddy the fields produce?"

He looked at me, then said, "Yes," in a thoughtful sort of way. "Yes, that makes sense."

"However," I went on, "the intense magnetic eddy also causes thunderstorms. And when the ghosts are strong enough to control it, they can tap the lightning."

Eakins scowled as he got the point. "Oh, we were lucky, weren't we? If that thing had started to feed off the thunderstorm last night it would have wiped this place off the face of the earth."

"Too right," I said.

He got up, took a drag on his cigarette, and said, "But I've got one to top that."

"What?" I said, standing and following him.

The others were already at breakfast in the big cool kitchen. Singh was staring at the crumbs of his toast and morosely stirring a cup of coffee. Everybody else seemed okay, except Colin, who had had his arm cut by flying window glass.

Eakins poured us coffee and sat down across the table from me. I said, "I'm listening."

He took a bit of paper from his jacket pocket, unfolded it, and passed it to me. It had a great long equation written on it. "There."

I read it, then I read it again, then once more to make sure I wasn't imagining it, and my stomach went all funny.

"Is that right?"

He sat back and folded his arms. "Me and the computer have been up all night arguing about it. That's the equation we agree on."

I looked at the paper again. "But what about radiation?" My stomach went funny again. I'd almost lain on top of that thing!

He shrugged. "I think the transplacement fields shielded us. You'd have been fried by hard X-rays if they hadn't."

34

Singh reached over and took the paper, read the equation. He looked up. "A black hole."

Eakins nodded. "I don't think it was ever really there, but it was gathering mass to become established. If Neil hadn't broken the link between the generator and the leys it would have become established and fallen straight through to the centre of the earth. Not a big one. An angstrom or two at best, but it'd be down there now, falling back and forth at the centre of the world, swallowing matter as it went. Off the top of my head, I'd say the world would have ceased to exist about a year from now if you hadn't done anything."

"Thanks," I said, feeling odd.

Singh got up from the table and went up the stairs.

Eakins watched him go. "Now what do you suppose is bothering him?"

"He gets upset very easily. You know why he was here at all?"

He nodded. "He wanted to talk to them."

"And it almost killed us all. He'll be all right."

Eakins reached over and retrieved the paper between thumb and forefinger. "Of course, the question now is, do we try again?" He looked at me from under his eyebrows.

"You have to be jesting," I said.

"We've still got plenty of money."

"That's not the point."

He raised an eyebrow.

"I'm making tracks right after dinner," I said. "What you do after that is on your own conscience, but don't try again."

"Isn't that passing the buck rather? It was all your idea in the first place."

"And I've got what I wanted. Brian, it's too dangerous to tamper with."

"We could learn to control it," he suggested.

"I hope that was a joke," I said. "It was only blind luck that that black hole didn't get established this time. Do you want to be responsible for the end of the world?"

He shook his head. "Okay, Neil. Ghosts go back to the ghost stories." He stretched slowly. "Can't say I'm really sorry, either."

I smiled. "Good lad."

Singh was sitting at the harpsichord in the music room, making up a pavane as he went along.

"It isn't the end of the world, Jim," I said.

He didn't stop. "It almost was."

I shrugged. "It wasn't, so why worry?"

He ended the music with a dissonant crash, turned to me. "Suppose one day a gate does that, Neil?"

"A gate only runs long enough to transmit or receive, you know that. The fields are never on for long enough. The generator was running continuously."

He waved his hands as he always did when trying to get an idea across. "Yeah, but *suppose*, Neil. Suppose one day, in Bogotá or Acapulco or Neasden, the conditions are exactly right at the exact moment a gate goes on, and the transplacement fields create a singularity."

I shrugged again. "End of the world, I suppose."

He scowled. "You're a bloody fatalist."

I smiled. "There are worse things to be."

"Look, can't you see the . . . the . . . frailty of all this? Okay, so it's a skillion-to-one chance that the conditions will ever be exactly right, but that skillion-to-one chance might drop tomorrow, or next week, or next year, or—"

"Or never. You know your problem? You've got a doom complex. The moment you got Kramer's theory straight in your head you instantly decided that the whole Universe isn't really there at all. Now you've decided the world's about to vanish up its own behind. Anything else you've forgotten? I mean, are we stripping the photosphere off the sun or something, or maybe draining the Earth's magnetic field away, or—" I stopped. He'd got that thoughtful look again.

I managed to get out of the door before he said anything.

the visible man

The car broke down three miles east of Kenmore. Melling scowled, let the Allegro run into the side of the road, put the handbrake on and got out.

sounded like the plugs

Nuts, he thought. He unlocked the bonnet, propped it open and blew out his cheeks with a banner of foggy breath. He didn't understand cars.

it's about time you started taking some notice of me

He bent under the bonnet and sighed. "Can't you shut up for a minute?"

it would be to your advantage if you started to listen to me

He straightened up, took out the prop and slammed the bonnet down. "No."

you're being unreasonable

He leaned back against the bonnet and lit a cigarette. "I'm not. You are." All around him hills stood bleak and empty against the fluffy grey clouds. Trees provided the only colour in the whole frosty landscape. He took a long drag, exhaled a cloud that was half smoke, half condensation. It all looked very lonely.

Up the road, a motor snarled. He turned with the cigarette halfway to his mouth, and watched a yellow breakdown truck come round the corner. He grunted and sat on the Allegro's bonnet as the truck slowed and stopped abreast of him.

"Good morning, Melling," said the driver, a bluff, cheery-looking man in a battered, faded tam o'shanter.

Melling didn't look at him. "Hello."

The truck's engine coughed, died, and the mechanic got out, took a toolbox off the passenger seat and slammed the door. "Now then, let's see those plugs."

Melling got off the bonnet, lifted it and propped it up. The mechanic took a plug spanner from his bag and took out one of the plugs. He held it up to the watery winter light and shook his head.

"How can you expect a car to work when the plugs are in this condition?" he said. "I keep on telling you to get a new car. I can give you any one you like. Jag, Merc . . ."

"It's my car, and I like it," Melling said.

The mechanic shook his head again. "Well I haven't any spare plugs on me at the moment. I'll give you a lift down to Killin."

"I wasn't going to stop in Killin."

"You could wait here."

Melling pursed his lips. "Yes, I could, couldn't I."

It took them about twenty minutes to drive through Kenmore and away along Loch Tay to Killin. The mechanic turned the truck in the forecourt of a small garage and switched off the engine. "Shan't be a minute," he said, getting out and vanishing into the dim interior of the garage beyond the double doors. Melling opened the passenger door and stood in the forecourt smoking another cigarette while he waited.

you're smoking too much

Push off, he thought.

it's like trying to talk to Portland Cement sometimes

Away on the oppressive hills the fluffy clouds were just beginning to spill down into the Tay valley. A snowflake drifted down from the sky and stuck to the concrete near his feet, then another.

38

An old woman with a shopping trolley went past the forecourt and waved to him. He didn't wave back.

The mechanic came out again with a box of plugs under one arm, looked up at the cloud. "There's a bad one coming," he commented.

"Think so?" said Melling.

The mechanic smiled. "I was right about the plugs, wasn't I?"

"You're always right," said Melling. "And it's getting bloody boring."

The mechanic chuckled. "You're always complaining," he said. "And that's getting bloody boring too."

Melling got in the truck. "Hard luck."

The clouds had boiled down into the valley by the time they got back to the car, and a sparse fall of snowflakes had begun, melting and running on the Allegro's bonnet and windscreen. The already thin, transparent light was beginning to fail, even though it was only about one in the afternoon, and some very dark snow-fluffy clouds were starting to peek over the hills. Melling stood watching them while the mechanic fitted the new set of plugs.

"It does look rough, doesn't it," the mechanic said without looking up.

"Get on with it," said Melling.

"You're getting rude too." But he didn't look at Melling.

"Understandable," Melling murmured to himself.

The mechanic came out from under the bonnet and wiped his hands on the front of his overalls. He took out the prop and closed the bonnet. "There, now don't let them get in that state again."

"No, mother."

The mechanic leaned in through the open window and turned on the ignition. The engine fired first go. Melling was getting fed up with the mechanic being right all the time.

"You shouldn't go on with a storm coming," said the mechanic. "The roads become blocked very easily."

Melling looked up at the clouds and wrinkled his nose. Maybe this time he should take his advice.

and about time too

There had been a morning, a while ago now, when Melling had woken up with a riot raging in his head. Millions of voices. Laughing, crying, singing, shouting, pleading. Love, hate, indifference, in hundreds of languages. The riot had quelled itself, the voices merging one by one. He'd almost gone mad that first morning, but when it was over, he found himself with something far worse . . .

The hotel looked nice on the outside, but Melling didn't like hotels. They were full of . . . them.

that's a blinkered old-fashioned way of thinking

The snow was blurring the day when he parked in the hotel car park. It was already a thin icing on the tarmac, settling thicker and thicker as he watched.

if you're thinking of going on, forget it

"I wasn't—"

I told you, the roads get blocked very easily

"I wasn't thinking that!"

okay, there's no need to shout; I can hear you

Melling opened the door, took his cases off the back seat. "Yeah, I know you can."

A woman was waiting at the desk when he pushed the doors open. She said, "Hello, Robert."

Melling put his cases down at the desk. "You know I don't like you to use my first name," he said, picking up the pen.

"I forgot," she said.

"I don't," he said, signing the book, "believe you."

"Shall I take your bags upstairs?"

He shook his head. "At least let me do some things for myself."

She nodded. "All right."

He stopped, stood for a moment, then dropped the cases. "No. You do it."

She came round the corner. "All right—"

"One of them in your teeth."

She looked at him a moment, then bent and took the handle of one of the cases in her mouth, straightened up slowly, and picked up the other, and slowly, painfully went up the stairs with them. Melling leaned on the counter and watched, trying to feel some sense of triumph, and failing. She came back down smiling that infuriating smile. "Anything else?"

"Get out of my head."

She just went on smiling and walked into the other room.

Upstairs, only one of the doors was open. His cases stood just inside the room; the covers of the bed had been turned down.

what did you do that for

"What?" He took off his coat and sat down on the bed.

making me carry that case in my teeth

"I didn't make you do anything."

you told me to

He lay back on the bed and closed his eyes. "You know what scares me? What scares me is that you're prepared to make yourself uncomfortable just because I say so."

I die every day; being uncomfortable is a little thing

"My heart bleeds for you."

you know, I still can't make you out

"You can spend the rest of eternity wondering." He sat up. "Leave me alone."

no

"Just for ten minutes, if I can pick the ten minutes. Just go away."

you know I can't do that

"Suppose I said I'd kill myself if you didn't go away?"

you forget that I know every little one of your psychoses and neuroses; suicide just isn't you, Melling

"Unreasonable stress . . ."

bull

"On the other hand, you might kill me with kindness."

oh, now you're just being silly

"Am I?"

you won't die; not if I can help it

Melling looked up. "Not if you can help it? Are you keeping me alive just for the laugh?"

at least try to be sensible; you're important to me, Melling

"You've an odd way of showing it."

I'm an odd person

Melling sighed and got up off the bed. Beyond the window the snow had blurred everything to an indistinct dirty drifting whiteness. "Too right," he murmured to himself.

For dinner he had quiche Lorraine, white wine, and coffee to follow, which certainly filled a hole, though he still slightly resented finding his favourite meals waiting for him everywhere he went.

"Suppose," he said to the waitress who came to clear the table, "I told you to have a war. A big one. A nuclear war."

She was in her twenties, prim and pretty and starched in blue and white. She shrugged. "There are some things I wouldn't do. And that's one of them."

"Yes, but you say you'll do anything to please me, keep me alive. So why not a war?"

She smiled. "The likelihood of you dying in a nuclear war would be rather high, wouldn't you say?" Melling sat back and drew on his cigar; the girl put plates on her tray. "I've had all the nuclear devices dismantled anyway. The plutonium and uranium are far more use in power stations. Besides, if I did have a war it'd kill millions. It'd be like you cutting off one of your legs."

Melling held up his cigar and looked at the glowing end. "There is of course the old story of the wildcat with its leg caught in a trap chewing the leg off to escape."

She picked up the tray, smiled. "You can never manage to get applicable analogies, can you?" she said. "Besides, if either of us is in a trap, it's not me."

That much was true. "No," he said. "No, I suppose you're not."

As she turned away she said, almost to herself, "Not while I have you, anyway," and Melling's stomach, not for the first time, went deathly cold.

The snow had stopped the next morning, but there was a great carpet of it over everything, several feet thick in places. It almost covered his car, and he reminded himself to get one of them to clear it. In the hotel, everything was snug and warm. In the dining room a grandmother clock beat a mechanical heartbeat while Melling ate breakfast alone. Bacon, egg, sausage, cereal, coffee. He still missed his morning paper, but not as much as he used to. He imagined that the world's news had become somewhat boring.

Abruptly, the door blew open and a gust of snowy air whipped in, frigid and scattered with flakes, and a bulky figure staggered into the foyer, fell full-length in front of the reception desk. The receptionist ignored it, went on reading her magazine as the springs forced the door shut again, sealing out the outside.

Melling jumped up and ran over to the figure, which was wheezing and panting from deep inside its thick clothing. Snow had soaked it through. He turned it over, took off the rucksack, unzipped the thick anorak and pulled the hood back. Long brown hair tumbled free. The receptionist didn't make a move.

"Get some blankets," said Melling.

The receptionist didn't move away from her magazine.

Melling stood up, grabbed her by the front of her blouse, pulled. Buttons popped, fell to the carpet. She looked up, and he repeated, "Get some blankets," very slowly.

She gave him a long cold look, then disengaged his fingers and walked away.

He bent down again, helped the girl to her feet. Her lips were blue with the cold, her teeth chattering. He helped her across to the fire and sat her down beside it, turned to see if blankets were on the way. The receptionist, the waitress and two maids stood just inside the room, watching. He stood up slowly.

"Why the hell don't you do something?" he shouted. He turned and looked at the girl, and her eyes met his, and he knew suddenly. "My God," he murmured. "She's not . . . she's . . ." The women remained motionless; he rounded on them. "That's it, isn't it! She's not part of you!"

One by one, the women turned and went out, the last closing the door quietly behind her.

"I thought I was the last sane person left in the world," the girl said, sipping her brandy. Her name was Alison, and the snow had caught her sheltering in a ruined barn out on the hills.

Melling smiled. "So did I. I've thought that for a long time."
who're you trying to kid
She put her glass down on the table and looked into the fire. "At first I wasn't even sure if I was sane any more," she said. "All those voices . . ." She shuddered.
He nodded. "That's how it was with me."
She rubbed her eyes. "And then there weren't so many voices. Then a few less, then a few less. Then there was just this one, and everyone I met knew my name . . . Then they stopped printing papers, and they stopped using money . . . I thought everybody had gone mad."
"Yes," he said. "Yes, I know how you felt."
She shook her head. "I still don't know what happened. The voice only ever spoke to me twice, then it . . . ignored me."
that's a lie; I just had other things to do
She sighed. "At first I thought maybe everybody had been taken over by something from outer space, but . . ." she shook her head again. "I don't know."
Relaxed now, he drew on his cigar. "No, nothing's come from outer space."
Her eyes brightened. "You know what's happened then?"
"Oh yes; my little voice seems to have spent more time with me than with you. It's been into a great deal of painful detail."
just so you understand, that's all
He took another drag on his cigar. "Everybody on Earth has become telepathic. I don't know how exactly, but it happened overnight; literally. Everybody's become part of a huge gestalt mind. Everybody, apparently, except you and me."
Her eyes narrowed. "Gestalt . . . ?"
He nodded. "One entity, one personality. Physically, everyone's still an individual. Mentally, they're all the same person. I'm still not sure if it's a very nice person either."
oh, you're just saying that
Melling smiled.
Alison said, "Then why aren't we part of this gestalt thing?"
He shrugged. "It knows; at least I assume it must. But it won't tell me."

"And the voice. That's the gestalt talking to us?"

as if it did any good

Melling nodded. "It looks as if it can still get inside us, even if our personalities can't become part of it."

She shuddered again. "It's awful."

He tapped ash from his cigar onto the carpet. Let them clear it up. "Oh, I don't know. There'll never be another war. No more crime or poverty."

if only you believed all that

"But it means no more individuality, doesn't it?" said Alison. "Just this one mind, in everyone's body. No more privacy. Even for us."

Melling nodded. "But there are still two of us outside it, so there's still some hope."

ah, but who for

She smiled. "Yes, there's still some hope."

It snowed again during the night, and the next morning his car was completely buried in the car park; just an indistinct lump. He stood scowling at the window. The Allegro would be ruined.

I hope you remembered to put some antifreeze in the radiator

"As if you'd ever let me forget."

it's the worst snowfall I've ever seen round here

Melling looked at the dirty yellow-grey sky. "I bet you've seen worse, though."

oh sure; Alaska, Norway, Antarctica; yes, I've seen worse

"Why didn't you help Alison yesterday?"

I have my own reasons

"Mm. I'll bet you do. And you never told me I wasn't the only person you were tormenting either."

I don't consider myself to be tormenting you

"You're ducking the question."

it wasn't a question; it was a statement

Melling frowned. "I was wondering last night about all the mental patients who became part of you. They must unbalance you a lot."

on the contrary, they lend balance; it would be a mistake to be too sane

He laughed. "I'll bet."

Alison wasn't in her room. The bed was made, the wardrobe and dresser empty, her rucksack and clothes gone. The moment he saw the empty room, Melling knew something bad had happened. He ran down the stairs.

"Where is she?" he shouted at the receptionist.

She didn't turn a hair; the smile was firmly in place. "Beg pardon?"

"Alison. Where is she? What have you done with her?"

She shook her head. "I don't know any Alison . . ."

Suddenly desperate, he leaned across the counter. "The girl who came in here yesterday."

She looked at the glass door, all steamed up. "In this weather . . .?"

He grabbed her blouse again, pulled hard until her nose almost touched his.

"Tell me where she is," he said quietly, forcing calm.

The smile never wavered. That was what got him very very mad. "I don't . . ."

The counter flap was open. He swung her round and through the gap, and her blouse tore in dozens of shreds. He pulled her to him, pushed back to his arms' length, and jerked hard, so that her head whipped back and forward. "Where is she?" he screamed.

"Robert . . ." Her hair was disturbed, the smile slipping.

"*Don't call me that!*" He pulled her to him again, and pushed her backward as hard as he could. She went through the glass door and fell back into the deep snow without a sound, her face suddenly expressionless. He only heard the sound of shattering glass a moment later.

"Melling!"

He turned slowly. The young waitress was standing beside the counter, face hard. "What have you done with her?" he shouted.

She stepped past him and stood in the ruin of the door. The

46

receptionist lay on her back in a hole in the snow, blouse ripped off, skirt up around her thighs. A dagger of glass over a foot long had gone right through her neck, and blood was pumping out of her, crystallising instantly into the snow. Her eyes were open, but she wasn't moving, and there was a terrible emptiness behind those eyes.

"Where—" The waitress whipped round and caught him back-handed across the face. He cried out and staggered back against the counter, holding his cheek.

"You bloody animal, Melling!" she yelled.

"You die every day," Melling sneered.

"Pointless, bloody murder!"

"So what? You can afford to lose one!"

She tore the prim white cap from her head, disturbing auburn hair. "Life is a precious thing, you bloody savage!"

"Alison's life too?"

The rage seemed to be sucked out of her. She sighed, deflated. "Get your coat. I'll show you where Alison is."

At some time the day before, or during the night perhaps, a path had been cleared through the snow. It had been covered during the night's fall, but it was still just about navigable. Wrapped in his RAF greatcoat, Melling followed the waitress through the snow, across the covered road, to the edge of the loch.

Before them, white hills sloped down onto a great unbroken sheet of white, as flat as a sheet of paper. They stood together on the shore and looked out across the snowfield.

"There are a lot of things I should have told you straight away," she said, each word a foggy balloon in the crisp, cold air.

"Yes," he said.

She put her hands in her pockets. "First of all, there are more people like you. Or rather there were."

He looked at her. "How many?"

She pursed her lips. "Several hundred. They're dead now. Some committed suicide, some had accidents, others just went mad and fell down dead. Some did terrible things when they realised the freedom they had. I had to kill them in the end."

"You never told me."

She looked out across the frozen lake. "You never really needed to know before."

"You never told me you were working on a need-to-know basis either."

She laughed a little cloud of fog. "There's a gene for telepathy, a dominant gene. Practically everyone has it, but it needs something to trigger it off and activate the sensitive areas of the brain, mainly in the right parietal lobe."

"You're succeeding if you're trying to blind me with science."

She shrugged. "It hardly matters. I'm not certain what triggered everyone off, but it happened one night last year, and a little later I developed consciousness. I don't think you realise how many people with the gene died too, how many couldn't stand the shock. It was a long . . . painful time."

"And I don't have this gene."

She shook her head. "Clears are very rare. That's why there were so few of you. In any major evolutionary advance there are bound to be a percentage of throwbacks. Whatever triggered everyone else, it didn't affect you."

He swallowed past a lump in his throat. "Alison."

She sighed and shook her head. "I can give you any woman you want, Melling; as many as you like. This one, for—"

"You've killed her."

She nodded at the loch. "Overdose of barbs in her bedtime milk; she just fell asleep. I had to use an acetylene torch to cut the ice. Three hundredweight of scrap to pull her down, and the hole just froze up twenty minutes after I'd finished. The wind chill factor must have been foul last night."

He closed his eyes, but the anger wouldn't come. "So it's an eye for an eye."

She looked across at him. "Oh, wake up, Melling . . ."

"So I'm the last human being on Earth now," he said quietly.

She scowled distastefully and shook her head.

"And you killed her because you were scared we'd have children, didn't you? Children who wouldn't ever be part of you. Seed of my loins, springing up to challenge you."

She smiled a genuine smile, like the sun coming out. "That's a rather flowery way of putting it," she said. "But yes, yes, that's what I wanted to stop happening. It was lucky that throwbacks were as rare as they were, otherwise there would have been two warring species on this planet. And believe me, Melling, you wouldn't have stood a chance."

"And suppose you had been the minority?"

"And every year that passed, there would be a few more telepaths, a few less clears, and sooner or later we'd be back here. It's useless to speculate."

He was silent a long time looking out over the loch before he said, "Why didn't you kill me too?"

She smiled. "And be rid of the problem once and for all? No. You've never understood, have you? In a world where I control everything, you're the only thing I can't predict, the last random factor. You're *interesting*."

That simple. "I'm not really flattered."

She looked at the ground, and stirred her toe in the snow. "Besides, you're the only person I've got left to talk to."

Melling turned and began to walk slowly away, suddenly feeling very tired.

"But be careful," she called after him. "I'm a jealous god."

He kept walking.

the
transplacement
trick

I hated mornings. Monday mornings in particular, and notably the first Monday of every month, when I went through the ridiculous ritual of trying to squeeze money out of a bureaucratic pinhead whom I'd never met and who was hotly antagonistic to my little world of computers and machines that transmitted matter to the far corners of the Earth.

Singh came past the door looking unreasonably bright and cheerful. "Good morning."

Rain pattered on the window; the inside of the glass was misty, probably from all the hot air coming up out of the phone. I banged the receiver down. "No it bloody isn't."

He backed up into the doorway, did one of his silly smiles. "Come on, smile for uncle Jimmy."

I scowled. "Stop being so bloody cheerful."

"Have you been talking to the men with the money again?"

I didn't say anything. One day I was going to find out the bureaucratic pinhead's gate number . . .

Singh crossed his arms and leaned against the door frame. "Let me guess."

"We can't have any more than our allocation, and even that may be cut soon. We're being strangled out of operation." I lit up a

Turkish fag; it was a habit I'd only just got back into, but I'd quickly come to depend on it again.

Singh sighed. "You should wait until you're awake enough to use your razor-sharp scientific wits to cut him down to size."

I looked at him through a cloud of cigarette smoke. "You're no help at all."

He sucked his teeth a bit, then said, "You'll get an ulcer if you worry too much."

"Someone has to worry." I blew out smoke; the fag was already making me feel better.

Singh shrugged. "I worry too."

I got up out of my comfy chair and walked round the desk. "Pull the other one."

In the next room, the big airy lab, we had set up eight separate full-scale gates and half a dozen half-size ones, scattered in groups of two and three across the lab. Rain drummed on the long skylights, loud in the silence of the big room. The lads weren't in yet. Singh and I walked slowly down the lab.

"They say we haven't learned much from all this," I said, nodding at the gear.

Singh looked around him. "They're right," he said.

I gave him my best hurt expression. "It's the principle of the thing, though. Scientific curiosity."

"Nowadays, scientific curiosity costs money. It's called inflation."

I stopped beside one of the experiments. Here, a powerful electromagnetic field made a gate transmit matter round corners. Maybe Singh was right. It was just a toy. "I am aware of the facts of life, thanks."

He grinned. "My, aren't we grumpy this morning. And you're smoking too many of those things too."

I looked at my cigarette. "Only because I'm upset." They were pricey too.

Down the lab, the big door rolled back and Len Bister stepped in from the rainy morning, dripping and sniffing.

"God, you two start early, don't you?" he said, shaking the rain off his coat. He hung it on a nail on the wall, took out a handkerchief and blew his nose. "Hell, I must be the only man who can catch a cold walking to the gate." Bister lived in Northampton and commuted to London to work every morning. It took him about five seconds to dial the gate to the lab, and maybe half a second to step through.

He plugged in the kettle and unlocked the coffee cupboard. "Alan phoned this morning. He can't make it for the next few days. He's got glandular fever or something." He put the catering-size tin of Nescafé on the bench and levered the top off with the handle of a spoon.

Singh grunted. "Glandular fever."

Bister squatted and searched the cupboard for his mug. "I think he said that anyway. It was a lousy line."

"Usually is from Inverness nowadays," said Singh. "Lines are in bad condition."

I sat down on a stool. "What we should have invented was a better telephone."

Bister looked at me, then at Singh. "What's bugging him?"

"He's been speaking to our benefactors again," said Singh.

Bister found his mug, shook a spider out of it, and stood up. "Oh." He spooned coffee into his mug. "I assume we aren't going to get our IBM 6069385 then."

I flipped the stub of my cigarette onto the concrete floor. "Too bloody right we're not."

"It's getting hard to arrange time-sharing nowadays," he said. "Universities are too busy doing their own thing and the big corporations won't allow independent groups access in case of industrial espionage."

"Yeah, I know," I said. "I know."

Paul Ewing, sheepskin coat glistening with rain, tatty at the shoulder and frayed round the buttonholes, looked round the door. "I keep telling you we should move to California, Neil," he said.

I looked at him. "Why is everybody so goddam happy today?"

He rolled the door shut behind him. "Climate's nicer in California," he said. "The facilities are better, and so's the bread."

"And where around here can you go surfing?" said Singh.

"Or get a suntan," said Ewing. "No offence, Jim," he added. Singh grinned.

I lit another cigarette. "Don't knock it, children. Everything's cool right here."

Bister looked around the lab. "Stop kidding yourself, Neil. It's dying on its feet."

"Kettle's boiling," I said. "Mine's two sugars."

"We're not making enough progress, that's the problem."

I hadn't been listening. "What?"

Singh put his glass down on the table. "We aren't making enough progress to keep their interest up. They won't pour money down a dead end for much longer."

Dim and rich, the Swan was slowly filling with the dinnertime crowd. I took a bite out of my pork pie, "Tough," I said.

"Eight big files full of notes," indicating the thickness with his hands, "and we're no closer to knowing how transplacement happens than when we found Preston's notes." He looked down at his beer. "What did you use to call it? An instrument that displaces matter if you build it . . . so and put a current through it, and a bunch of outside factors that disturb its operation. That's still all it is; all we've done is find some more outside factors."

I stared at the crumbs of my pie. He was right, of course. He was spending a lot of time being right just lately, but I wouldn't admit it. "NASA doesn't know, CalTech doesn't know, the Russians don't know. They've made less progress than we have, but they get money and instruments and personnel and places to work and . . ."

"We ought to defect."

I laughed. The words Iron Curtain and Bamboo Curtain were just historical terms now; transplacement had made it impossible for them to exist; the Berlin Wall was just a big stack of brick. A world united by its instantaneous travel system, and nobody had a clue how it worked. I assumed that Preston had known, but that wasn't much good because he'd died before he could tell anyone. Singh and I had come up later and pirated his notes detailing an electronic instrument which transmitted matter, without a mention of how it did it.

"If we found out how it worked they'd be beating a path to our door. Nobel prizes all over the place, no sweat."

Singh pulled a face at me. "Can't you be satisfied with one?"

"I'll bet Crick and Watson didn't work in a converted garage after they got their prize," I said moodily.

He grinned an ivory grin. Somebody jogged my shoulder as they made their way to a free table. I took another mouthful of bitter and swallowed in a satisfied way. The Swan was insulated, far away from the troubles of the world, a little bubble of calm full of beer and cigarette smoke. Sitting there, I could almost imagine I was back in the old days before we found Preston's notes, back when I was earning a steady wage as an experimental physicist and being nasty to all the research assistants, back before we had visited transplacement on the unsuspecting world. Outside, there would be cars on the street again instead of weeds poking up from the road surface. Cars puthering out lots of lovely lethal carbon monoxide and delightful amounts of lead compounds and sulphur. At least then the air smelled interesting, even if it did give you asthma and bronchitis and God knows what else. And traffic jams! You never miss anything until it's gone forever. I'd *enjoyed* traffic jams! There were times when I didn't like the brave new world we'd helped to drag into being.

Somebody tapped me on the shoulder, and I came out of it. "Er, please excuse me."

I shifted my stool, thinking that he wanted to get past, but he just stood there with his hands clasped together. He looked about thirty, but his curly hair was receding up his forehead. He wore a tatty brown jacket over a tattier blue cardigan and white shirt and tie with a microscopic knot. He wore wire-rimmed spectacles and looked the archetypal mad scientist, all nervous and apologetic.

"Please excuse me," he said again, and his uneven teeth were yellow, "but are you Dr Neil Judson?"

I nodded. "That's right."

The clasped hands parted for a moment, then clasped again. "You know, when I heard you had taken the premises around the corner, I couldn't believe it. Ah, may I sit down?"

Singh and I looked at each other, and he shrugged slightly. I said, "Yeah, sure."

He pulled up a stool and sat with both thin, white hands folded in his lap. "You know, when I was a boy, matter transmission was a thing only to be found in science fiction, and you in less than five years have made it a reality." He shook his head reverently. "It's a great, wonderful thing."

Singh and I exchanged glances again. Singh said, "It's nice to know that somebody appreciates us," without bothering to mention how we'd conned NASA into doing all the vital development by selling transplacement as the gateway to the stars.

"Can we help you, Mr . . .?" I asked.

"Walter Ellis."

"What can we do for you, Walter?" I asked. I had to work hard to stop myself laughing.

He did a little bounce on his stool. "Oh no, it's rather what I can do for you."

Singh put his elbow on the table and rested his chin on his hand and put on his Look Of An Interested Genius. "Oh yes, Mr Ellis?"

He was off in a wave of enthusiasm. "Oh yes, yes. I do hope you won't think I was prying, but I couldn't help overhearing your conversation, and I can definitely help you."

I put both elbows on the table and leaned towards him and in a very grave voice said, "How exactly, Mr Ellis?"

Singh almost cracked out laughing.

Ellis didn't notice. He recrossed his hands, like two white birds nesting in his lap, and said, "I know what makes transplacement work."

Ellis lived around the corner from the Swan, in a shabby street full of empty, broken-windowed houses. It was Singh's idea to go with him.

At the end of the street, beside the towering legs of a useless railway bridge, Ellis stopped and took a key from his pocket. The key opened the grimy front door of a shabby, dirty house. Kids had been down the street with spraycans and hadn't noticed that the end house was still occupied. The colour didn't help the surroundings.

The front door opened into a dim musty hall covered with greasy wallpaper. Ellis led the way up the hall, talking as he went.

"I first became interested late last year, when the gate on the corner failed—do you know that the weather affects them sometimes? Yes, you must do. Anyway, the men who came to repair the gate showed me the diagrams and all the equipment. You know, it really is a simple device when you come down to it."

"Isn't it," said Singh.

"Anyway, it occurred to me that the basic design could be improved on, and in so doing I discovered the principle behind it."

"You built your own gate?" said Singh.

"Oh yes, certainly."

"You do know it's patent protected," I said.

He stopped and looked round. "Oh?" He seemed genuinely surprised.

I shrugged. "Skip it."

It stood in the little kitchen, a man-high gateway of tubular construction, on a metal base. Two wires were . . . I bent down and had a good look. The bared ends of the wires were Sellotaped to the metal base. And there was something else wrong too. I tapped the tubing gently, and the whole thing rocked. It was cardboard, sprayed silver. Ellis had built his gate out of old toilet roll tubes. Singh blinked.

I swallowed. "Does it, um, work?"

Ellis nodded. "Oh yes, yes."

Singh scratched the side of his nose and said, "Could we, er, see it in, um, action?"

"Oh certainly, certainly." Ellis's face lit up like a lighthouse. He took a box from a cupboard, plugged the two wires from the gate into it, and plugged the box into a socket over the cooker. The box was an old cornflakes packet, but he held it as if there was something heavy inside, and there were two red buttons poking out through holes in the side. He plugged two more wires from the box into sockets in the cardboard uprights of the gate, then turned on the socket, pressed one of the red buttons and put the box down on the kitchen table.

"It takes a moment to warm up," he apologised with a nervous smile.

"I'll bet it does," I murmured. Singh nudged me in the ribs.

"I should perhaps explain that the gateway is only there to mark the outline of the field. My generator does not need the conductance offered to your version by the metal gateway. It's a sort of trans-placement gate without the corners."

Without the corners. "Mm," I said.

He looked at his watch. "It should be ready now," he said, and reached across and pressed the other red button and stepped up to the gate. Singh and I exchanged knowing glances, and then Ellis stepped smiling through the gateway and suddenly wasn't there any more.

Singh's jaw dropped so far it almost broke on the floor. "Well I'll be damned," he said.

We stood for ages just looking at Ellis's gate before I went over and carefully opened the end of the cornflakes packet. Inside were two PP11 radio batteries and three circuit boards stacked neatly on top of one another. I burst out laughing, because it was so absolutely bloody marvellous that this little man living in a hovel had built a gate out of toilet roll tubes, turned it on, and got it to work. In a minute Ellis would come back and tell us the marvellous secret he had stumbled on. I went straight on laughing because it was so incredible.

Singh wasn't laughing. He looked as if someone had snuck up behind him and plugged him into Battersea power station. He looked at me, eyes staring, and I stopped laughing.

"Where's he *gone*, Neil?" he said quietly.

treasure trove

The night was dense and watery, whipped cold by a razor of a wind. The car made slow, difficult progress up the steep, wet road winding painfully up the face of the hill and onto the moor. Rain lashed in jewelled cones of headlight; even over the noise of the labouring engine Cooper could hear the wind scream against the car. The heater wasn't doing a very good job, and he sank down further into his coat. In the driving seat Sergeant Line squinted between the beating wipers and tried to keep the car on the unfenced road.

The road finally crested the hill, and the engine note changed as the car reached the flat. Sergeant Line changed gear, looked across at Cooper. "Not far now."

"It's a foul night," said Cooper.

Sergeant Line changed gear again. "It is indeed, Mr Cooper. It is indeed." He took a hip flask from the glove compartment, handed it to Cooper. Cooper flipped the top back and took a sip. Brandy, warm and mellow.

"I don't expect you're very pleased to come out on a night like this," he said.

Line smiled. "Part of my job, sir. I'd be out anyway; somebody broke into an electrician's in the village just before you got here. I'd only be out chasing him." He nodded through the windscreen. "That's it."

Bright it was, flickering in the driving rain, and for a moment he thought it was a factory or something. A fluorspar mine perhaps, or an oil refinery; a misty double line of jewelled lights. The moment passed. The line of lights was embedded in the ground at an angle of about twenty degrees.

Sergeant Line pulled the panda car to a stop and turned off the engine. In the sudden silence the noise of the wind seemed much much louder, an awful, almost-solid thing. Line did up his overcoat and put on his cap, pulling the brim down to his eyebrows, and looked at Cooper. "All right?"

Cooper buttoned his trenchcoat and turned the collar up. "Yes."

The cold was like a razor; it sliced through his coat and cut down to his bones; wind and rain tore at his face, stung the skin. On the other side of the car Sergeant Line, face screwed up against the wind, closed the driver's door and turned his collar up. He looked across the slick roof at Cooper and grinned. Cooper didn't see; he only had eyes for the great thing out on the moor.

In the sodden dark, he could just see a great scar on the moor where grass and heather had been torn up and ploughed aside. His eyes couldn't find the end of it; it must have been over a quarter of a mile long. At the near end of the gouge was a great dark thing, outlined only by the double row of lights and the strange shape it made against the barely lighter sky. His eyes were fooled by the odd angle for a moment, but the image suddenly sorted itself out. A great flat disc, stuck in the ground at a shallow angle, its rim ringed with a double line of tiny, very bright lights. It looked like a huge bejewelled poker chip, flipped carelessly to the ground.

Cooper took a long, long breath and tried to stay calm. Line came up beside him with his hands in his pockets and water dripping from the brim of his cap. "Wonder where it's from," he said.

"How many people know it's here?" said Cooper.

"You, me, two of my men, the man who found it. Five of us."

He tore his eyes from the thing, turned to Line. "Have you got the man who found it?"

Line nodded; water cascaded off his cap. "His name's Naughton. He was just driving across the moor when he saw it. He was trying to find the Manchester road. He's back at the station."

Cooper nodded. He'd have to have a long chat with Mr Naughton. Later, though. First, the wonderful thing that stood there in the wind and rain and dark.

"Has anyone touched it?" he asked as they strode across the wet heather.

"No," said Line.

"Any recent reports of lights in the sky? Flying saucers? Little green men?"

Line's eyebrows went up at the last, but he didn't comment. "Not a thing. It might as well have come here on the back of a lorry."

Unlikely, Cooper decided. It was difficult to say at the moment, but the disc looked to be between a hundred and a hundred and fifty yards across, though the angle at which it had buried itself in the ground was awkward and made it hard to judge. If it wasn't an extremely elaborate hoax, it must weigh several hundred tons.

"Noises then. Somebody must have heard it come down; it must have been going at a hell of a clip to bury itself like that." He looked at the great scar which ran away into the driving dark behind the thing. "It must have been trying to land."

"It made it," said Line. "No, we didn't have any reports yesterday or the day before. There was a bad thunderstorm here last night."

"Damn," said Cooper.

"Does it matter?"

Cooper shrugged. "Every little helps."

Line nodded. "I'll make enquiries."

They avoided the gouge the disc seemed to have made, and walked round until they stood beside the thing, and Cooper realised it was much larger than he had first thought. More like two hundred and fifty yards across. It must weight a couple of thousand tons. It had driven something like half its length into the ground, as if it was trying to bury itself out of sight. Ahead of it, the moor had piled up like a breaking wave.

"Someone must have heard something," Cooper said. "This thing would have come down like an earthquake."

Line shrugged. "I wasn't here last night. Like I said, I'll make enquiries."

Here beside it, Cooper was uncomfortably conscious of the presence of the great machine, alien and overpowering. The lights, bright and steady, seemed to signal somehow the power within, and looking at them in this desolate place made him feel cold inside. It didn't belong here . . .

"Is it safe to get this close?" said Line.

Cooper shrugged. "Maybe it is, maybe it isn't. Somebody has to look at it."

"People have been burned getting too close to them, haven't they?" said Line.

Cooper sniffed and buried his hands in his pockets. "I'm not supposed to say anything about that."

Line nodded to himself. "Thought not."

Cooper looked at him. "Sergeant, when we get back to the village you're going to sign a document for me which makes it a treasonable offence to release this information to anyone not cleared through me."

Sergeant Line looked him in the eye. "You're serious, aren't you?"

"Oh yes, Sergeant, I'm serious."

Line looked at the ship, shrugged. "Makes no odds." He nodded his head. "I reckon that's a door."

It took Cooper a moment to locate it among the other lights: a little square lighted cavity in the hull, about ten feet from the ground. Cooper stepped up to the hull and put his hand down flat on the metal. Cold and smooth, black as sin. How far had it come, though . . .?

There were some rungs recessed into the metal under the door. Rather close together, but obviously functional. Cooper looked up at the beckoning doorway, then started to climb. He swung his leg over the rim of the doorway, and stepped in.

The room was tiny, just big enough for three men to stand crushed up inside; the ceiling was just six feet from the floor, and he had to stoop. The three walls were blank, save for a fat red button about four feet from the floor on one wall, surrounded by a red painted square.

Line's head came up over the edge of the door, looked about, then surged up into the little room. Cooper looked round. "Sergeant . . ."

Line shook rain from his cap. "If I'm going to sign your paper, I want to know what it is I'm protecting."

Cooper nodded. "Okay, Sergeant, it's your choice." He looked about him. This must be an airlock, with the ceiling so low. In that case the fat red button in the wall must be . . .

He frowned at the button. "You know, Sergeant Line, I'm not really authorised to do this."

Line laughed. "That's all right, Mr Cooper. Neither am I."

Cooper smiled and bent down and pressed the red button. It went in easily, and he felt it click.

The outer door came down like a guillotine, sealing them in. Line looked round, then back at Cooper. Neither of them said anything. There was a quiet hissing from somewhere, and Cooper felt his ears pop. The air in the airlock grew warm, and Cooper felt the first tiny fingers of claustrophobia start to trip through his mind. It suddenly occurred to him that they might not breathe real air . . .

Abruptly, the wall slid upward, opening the airlock into a low corridor. The air was warm, but dry, at a slightly greater pressure than outside, but it smelled all right. Cooper stepped out unbuttoning his coat and looked both ways along the corridor. Line stepped out beside him and blew out his cheeks. "They like it hot, anyway," he said, undoing his coat and flapping it about.

Cooper sniffed the air. Yes, it did smell okay. "I'm just glad they breathe the same sort of air as we do."

Line looked up and down the corridor. "Which way do we go?"

Cooper pointed the way Line was looking. "That seems as good a way as any."

The corridor turned out to be circular, running around the ship. A quarter of an hour brought them back to the airlock. They had found three radial corridors leading inboard from the circular one, and they started down the nearest. It crossed two other circular corridors, and then went down a flight of steps and ended in a wall with a large square window in it. Cooper put his forehead against the window and looked in. He had to bend slightly.

Beyond the wall were long lines of large boxes, each with a big pair of silver catches attached to the lid. Huge boxes, like big freezer cabinets. Row after row after row of them in the dimly-lit room beyond the wall. Cooper frowned. Now what in hell were they?

There was a spiral staircase beside the wall, turning up through the low ceiling into the level above. Line came down the last turn shaking his head. "There's just a blank wall at the top," he said.

Cooper looked up. "It might be the control room," he said. "They wouldn't leave the key in the door."

Line nodded. "Mm."

Cooper looked back through the window, and realised suddenly what the cabinets must be for. It made him take a quick breath, shocked. What they'd stumbled on was beyond anything from a Norse longbarrow, more precious than anything of the Egyptians.

It was a cargo ship.

Back in the village they bought each other stiff drinks to warm the ice out of their bones, and it helped warm the chill out of Cooper's heart. A cargo ship. It could be carrying anything. Textiles, treasure, weapons, tools, scientific instruments—any one of the things in that hold was a potential revolution, simply because it hadn't originated here. The ship itself was beyond price. Cooper suddenly realised he was shaking.

"What now?" said Line, who didn't seem in the least disturbed by all this.

Cooper looked at his glass. His throat was dry, his eyes ached. He shook his head. "I don't know; I can't think clearly." He felt like screaming. Something was bottled up inside him and he wanted to yell it all over the pub, to run screaming in the streets and tell the world of the wonderful, terrible thing that had come here. And he couldn't; it was the very thing he was here to stop.

"Perhaps you're catching cold," said Sergeant Line.

He gulped down his Scotch. "Perhaps I am."

"What about the people from the ship?"

Cooper scowled. He'd hardly given any thought at all to the crew. He hadn't expected them to survive a crash like that, but someone (or something) had got out and left the airlock open. And was even now wandering aimlessly (or with some nameless alien purpose) on a strange world. Scared, disoriented, injured maybe; carrying God only knew what kind of weapons. Cooper started to feel cold again.

"Shall I have my lads look out for little green men?" said Line.

He shrugged. "I don't know what good it'd do."

"You don't want them running about the country scaring everybody, do you?"

Cooper shook his head. "It's one of the last things we want."

Line nodded. "All right then. Shouldn't be too difficult to find them. I mean, it isn't likely that they look much like us, is it?"

Cooper thought of the low corridors, that claustrophobic airlock. "One thing's certain, they're smaller than we are."

"Little green men then?"

"Green, blue, red, purple, gold . . ." Cooper shrugged. "Orange?"

"I get the idea," said Line, nodding. He stood up and pushed his chair back from the table. "I'll ring the station now."

Cooper nodded. "All right." But Line didn't move. Cooper looked up, but Line was looking past him, at the door of the public bar. Cooper was suddenly aware that the pub had become awfully quiet. Unnaturally quiet. He turned and looked towards the door, and his heart froze in his chest.

He looked as if he had been carved from a tree trunk; five feet high and three wide, blocky and squat. His golden hair hung, fine and silky, down to the small of his back, blowing in the wind which came through the door he held open with one huge gloved hand. He wore a black quilted jumpsuit, black boots and a quilted helmet with some kind of mike on it. Over one shoulder he had a big coil of heavy cable.

"Hello," he said.

They took the alien back to the police station and sat him down in the interrogation room. Cooper was beginning to feel worse. His eyes hurt more, and the pain was building up a knot of agony in his forehead. He had an argument with Line about whether the police should be here at all, and Line pointed out that Cooper was, after all, using police property. Cooper left it, and turned on the alien, who had been sitting quietly with a slightly amused expression on his face.

"Can you understand me?" Cooper asked very slowly.

The alien nodded. "Yes, I understand you," he said in perfect English. Craggy face: broad, flat nose, heavy eyebrow ridges, deep-set yellow eyes, square jaw, small mouth, blocky cheekbones. The hair was wrong on a head like that. It should have been cropped close to the skull, but it cascaded golden on his shoulders, rippled against the black jumpsuit. He had taken off the helmet mike.

Cooper barely managed to fight down the shock to ask, "Where did you learn our language?"

"There are ways." The alien's voice boomed in the great deep barrel of his chest.

Cooper felt lost, drowning. "What's your name?" And the moment he said it, he felt the inanity of the question. He suddenly felt very silly, and somewhat savage.

The alien didn't seem to notice. "Aldreth," he said. "Aldreth Spiermin-Haytha Ring."

Cooper leaned forward. "Where are you from, Aldreth?" And that sounded even more inane than the previous question.

The small, straight mouth twitched up at one corner. "I reserve the right to answer that question."

"You scared a lot of folk tonight," said Sergeant Line. Unimpressed.

Aldreth shrugged. "I did not mean to. I am sorry."

"Why did you come in the pub in the first place?" asked Line.

"Curiosity," said Aldreth. "If curiosity counts as an excuse here."

Line smiled. "Did you break into an electrician's shop tonight?"

Cooper sighed. "Sergeant . . ."

Aldreth smiled again, no doubt sensing dissent in the ranks of the enemy. He said, "I am afraid I did force entry into a shop selling electrical goods. You have me there."

"And the cable," said Line.

"I left payment," said Aldreth. "The cable is necessary for repairs to my ship."

"How many of you are there?" said Cooper.

"There is only one of me," said the alien. "As you can see."

"Cut the comedy," said Cooper.

Aldreth leaned his great blocky body forward. "Where I come from, it is protocol to inform one when an interrogation begins," he said, and the deep rumbling voice was like the noise of an iceberg breaking free of a glacier.

Cooper took a long breath. The eyes, yellow and hard as a jonquil diamond, locked unblinking to his, taunting him to lose his cool, slightly amused. He let the breath out and sat back slowly. It had been a close thing. Aldreth smiled again.

"So what brings Aldreth Ring to Earth?" Line asked casually.

The yellow eyes flicked to the policeman. Policeman's instinct; Line had rattled the alien. Aldreth said, "Aldreth Spiermin-Haytha Ring, if you please," and his voice had a slight edge it hadn't had before. Cooper hoped the alien wouldn't lose his temper; even though he was about sixteen inches taller than Aldreth, he didn't relish the idea of fighting him. He looked as if he had been born on a planet with a heavier surface gravity than Earth. Which would account for his squat, muscular body and the higher air pressure in his ship. Cooper watched as Aldreth sat back, ran a finger along a seam of his glove. The seam parted under his finger and he pulled the glove off. He repeated the action with the other hand. Cooper watched, almost mesmerised. The secret of the gloves alone would be worth millions to the clothing industry.

Aldreth brushed a ripple of hair from his face with an almost effeminate gesture. His fingers were long and slender, and the nails were blue. Painted. On the right index finger was a big chunky gold ring set with sparkling green stones. Cooper looked at the alien again, and realised that Aldreth was wearing ear-rings.

"You're a merchant," said Cooper.

Aldreth nodded slightly like a player acknowledging a point to an opponent. "Well guessed."

"A rich merchant. Rich and fat and inept."

Aldreth stopped smiling, but he said, "In this business, one grows neither rich nor fat by ineptitude."

Cooper felt his headache start to slip away. That was twice they had managed to rattle Aldreth. They were slowly gaining the advantage.

"Am I free to go now?" asked Aldreth.

"No you bloody well aren't," said Line.

Aldreth nodded at the coil of heavy cable, which lay in one corner. "I wish to repair my ship and be gone from this wretched place, that is all," he said. "What can you hope to gain by keeping me here?"

Cooper looked at Line, who raised an eyebrow. He didn't know either.

"Suppose we won't let you go?" said Line.

"That would be an unfortunate move," said Aldreth.

"Why?" said Cooper.

Aldreth crossed his arms stuffily and didn't answer.

Cooper got up and paced around the table until he was behind Aldreth. He put his hands on the alien's great hard shoulders, but Aldreth made no move. Cooper said, "Aldreth, where you come from, is it legal for a merchant to land on a savage planet like ours?"

Aldreth's head half-turned, stopped. He didn't say anything. Cooper jumped on the confirmation.

"Because that's what you were going to do, isn't it? You were going to come here and unload your wares on us. Stolen, are they?"

A short, sharp intake of breath. Aldreth had underestimated them. "Conjecture," he said.

"Oh, I don't think so," said Cooper. "There's no such thing as a one-day language cram course, even for you. You intended to come here all along, and you learned our language to deal with us."

"Then why is my ship stuck in the ground like that?"

"You made a mistake."

Aldreth shook his head slightly. "The mistake is yours."

Cooper knelt down beside the chair. "I don't think so, Aldreth. We've got the jump on you, and there's nowhere for you to go. Level with us, Aldreth."

Aldreth thought about it a moment, then said, "If you do not allow me to return to my ship and repair certain damage, I cannot be held responsible for the consequences."

"What consequences, Aldreth?" Cooper pressed. "We can't help if we don't know what's going on."

Aldreth's head turned, and the yellow eyes bored into his own. "If I am not allowed to repair my ship, your world will cease to exist. Do you want to be responsible for that?"

Aldreth explained it as well as he could in the car. The ship's drives had suddenly, inexplicably failed as it had entered the Earth's atmosphere, leaving him with attitude drives only. Since artificial gravity maintained the interior of the ship at three-quarters the gravity he was used to, the crash hadn't killed him, and he'd baled out in great haste in case the thing blew up. It didn't, and he ventured inside again to see what he could do to repair things. And that was when he discovered a bad thing.

The main drive moved the ship from star to star by somehow relaxing local space and enabling the mass to slip from one mathematical domain to another. Aldreth wrote a lot of equations for him on the back of an envelope, but he couldn't understand them. He put them in his pocket until he could give them to someone who would.

There was something wrong with the main drive. It was turned up to full intensity and jammed there, and a countdown had been initiated which he was unable to stop. When the main drive went on it would relax a region of space some four miles in diameter, and twenty-eight seconds later the Earth would be turned inside-out.

"My computers predict it will take that long for the domain to create critical stress," said Aldreth.

"How long have we got?"

Aldreth was quiet a moment, converting numbers. "Twenty minutes."

Cooper looked at Line, who nodded. "It'll be all right."

"I am not even certain I can repair the damage," Aldreth said. "I am not an engineer."

"This is a fine time to tell us," said Line.

"It is a difficult thing to do, and I am not as well-conversed with computers as I used to be."

"Well we can't do it," said Line.

Aldreth looked at his hands. The big, blocky brows drew together. "The relaxation will not stop here," he said. "It will expand to take in your sun and every planet in this solar system, and when it reaches critical size the domain will collapse and form a singularity."

"A black hole," said Cooper.

"A black hole," said Aldreth.

"Sounds a bloody dangerous thing to be driving about in," said Line.

Aldreth shrugged. "In normal circumstances the relaxation only occurs for a millionth of a second, out in space far from any planet, and the domain only extends a little further than the hull of the ship. It is perfectly safe in normal circumstances."

Line grunted and drew the car to a stop. Aldreth took the coil of cable from the floor and opened the door. He jumped out into the rain and wind, and took off at a run towards the ship. Cooper opened the door on his side. "You stay here," he said to Line. Line made a face, but didn't protest.

He caught up with Aldreth at the bottom of the ladder. The alien stopped with one foot on the bottom rung. "You cannot help."

"Doesn't matter."

He followed the alien up the ladder and into the airlock, then down the corridor and one of the radial corridors, down two sets of steps, to a blank wall. Aldreth waved a hand in the air, and the wall slid upward.

"You must not come in here," he said to Cooper. "The ship knows me, and your presence here could be fatal."

"I think you just don't want me to see the drive."

"Think what you wish, you may not come in here." He turned through the doorway, and the wall came down before Cooper could move. Cooper pulled a face and swore at himself for letting the alien get that far in front of him. He banged on the wall.

"Aldreth!" The wall was solid, seamless. "Damn you, Aldreth, open this thing!" He bared his teeth and leaned his forehead against the wall. It was warm, slightly rough-textured. "Oh, hell fire," he murmured. The alien could be doing anything in there. Anything at all. All that power . . . "Damn."

A quarter of an hour had never seemed so long. In the end he got fed up with pacing about and sat down on the steps, head in hands, and worried a lot.

"Are you ill?"

He looked up. Aldreth was standing in the doorway with his arms crossed, leaning on the frame. Cooper hadn't heard the door go up. "You locked me out."

The great chunky face cracked into a grin. "What is your name?"

"Cooper."

"The thing about you, Cooper," Aldreth said as the door closed behind him, "is that you worry about all the wrong things."

"Have you fixed it?"

"To use the vernacular, no sweat."

"The world isn't going to end?"

Aldreth stepped towards him. He didn't have the coil of cable any more. "I shouldn't think so."

Cooper stood up. "What did you do?"

"Another worrying habit you have is asking too many questions." The alien tapped him warmly on the back as he went past up the steps. "Enjoy life, Cooper. Stay cool." He let the word trail off. *Cooool.*

Cooper grinned slowly and followed him.

"You were close when you guessed I was here to trade stolen goods with you," Aldreth said as they made their way up the corridor. "The goods are stolen, though I myself did not steal them. I was coming here to hide them. And myself, come to that. Do you think I could pass as a native?"

Cooper shrugged and tried to picture Aldreth in a business suit, or denims. "I suppose so. If you had your hair cut."

Aldreth touched one long thick silky tress and wrinkled his nose.

"You could stay here," Cooper prompted hesitantly.

Aldreth looked at him and grinned. "I see right through you, Cooper, as clear as the air."

Cooper shrugged. "What would you do in my position?"

Aldreth shook his head slightly. "I am sorry, Cooper. I am a merchant, and used to seeing ulterior motives. Merchants' nose, we call it."

They were at the airlock. "Well at least we trust each other now."

Aldreth shook his head again. "Fatal error in this profession. No, Cooper, my secret is out; I cannot stay here. I shall have to find somewhere else to hide." He sighed, shrugged.

"Are there many other planets like Earth?"

Aldreth started to answer, then put on a sly smile. "Information is a tradeable commodity."

"You can't stop trying to make money can you, you greedy little sod."

"It is an attitude which befits the job."

Cooper put his hand against the airlock door. "Aldreth, if you leave some of your cargo here as a gesture of good faith, I'll promise you sole trading rights to Earth."

Aldreth frowned and pursed his lips. "Are you in a position to make such a promise?"

"No, of course I'm not, but I can talk to people who can talk to people who are. They'll jump on the idea."

Aldreth shook his head. "Not good enough, Cooper. I need personal representation, even for a contract of good faith."

"Wait a while then."

"I am a somewhat excitable person. I had best be away from here soon." His forehead wrinkled deeply in thought for a moment. "Look, if I come here again on open trading terms, will you promise not to tell anyone about this matter?"

Cooper felt his stomach do a little jump. "Sure," he said in a whisper. Then louder. "Sure."

"I shall want a small group of your businessmen to have terms ready and a trading programme drafted out for us to work on when I come here again. I shall not agree to make any trade in weapons with you. Can you do that?"

Cooper nodded dreamily. "Yes. Yes, right."

"And negotiations must be made through you. In the early stages I will deal through no one else. Do you understand?"

It was like a fairytale happening around him. "Yes."

"If of course I do come back," Aldreth added thoughtfully, half to himself.

"If." And the dream, bright and sharp, began to shatter.

"I have not endeared myself to the authorities. I am handling stolen goods, trading illegally, as you surmised. I am already wanted for evasion of port dues, import tax, export tax . . ." He shrugged. "One cannot operate at optimum profit within the boundaries of the law. If I am lucky, and things do cool off, I will come back. It could be several years, though."

"How many's 'several'?"

Aldreth shrugged again. "But you have my word that I shall return." A small smile. "One cannot turn down the opportunity of sole rights to a new market."

"I thought not," Cooper said.

"As a mark of personal goodwill, you can have anything you choose from my hold."

Arrested, the dream, though flawed, was still in one piece. "Right."

It was still raining when Line helped him lift the crate down out of the airlock. Aldreth had told them to get well out of the way, so they loaded the crate onto the back seat of the panda car, got in and drove off the moor and down the hill. Looking out of the rear window, Cooper saw something bright and rain-jewelled fill the sky behind them. The headlights dimmed, the engine coughed, Line swore quietly. Cooper held his breath for an eternal moment, then the bright thing flipped away into the night and rain, and the engine caught again.

Cooper looked at the little crate on the seat beside him. It seemed to be of a light alloy, painted pastel yellow, its corners and edges rounded. There had been thousands just like this in the lockers in the hold. Anything could be inside, but whatever it was, its extraterrestrial origin would cause a revolution. It might give him the power to destroy continents, or cure cancer, change the world, alter the course of technical advance. He'd picked completely at random, and Aldreth hadn't tried to influence him.

There were words stencilled blue and small on the lid of the crate, set out in an efficient, neat way in a language he couldn't understand, in letters which were totally unfamiliar to him in shape. But he'd expected that. He reached up and turned on the interior light. Line looked round at the sudden illumination, then went back to keeping the car on the road.

Cooper put his hands flat on the top of the crate, flipped the blue clasps up with his thumbs, and lifted the lid slowly to reveal the wonder inside.

The interior of the crate was sectioned like a beer crate. The overhead light, though weak, flashed on cut crystal, on dull glowing copper, bright silver. Cooper sat stunned at the beauty of the things for almost a minute before realising what they were, and after a moment a chuckle bubbled its way up from his chest and became a low laugh, and in the back of the car he sat back and burst out laughing.

The crate was full of candlesticks.

abyss

First, the colours. Shades of grey and dark green swimming in the early mists. From the crest of the hill one could look out over the dark vale, knotted with trees seemingly afloat on the mist, and dark and far-away mysterious, the rough edge of the curling crest of the Downs. Trees: skeletal, filled in black and blue with a ruined pen against pastel blue and grey touched by orange morning.

Shades on, the man came jogging easily down the sweep of deserted motorway in the quiet dawn. Far ahead a knot of colour amid grey and green descried a village, and on the hill above it a solitary group of trees, gaunt-legged and fuzz-headed, stood sentinel over the silent world.

The man jogged slowly to a stop and rested a moment to check his map from the rucksack he carried on his back. He located the village, but its name meant nothing to him. It hardly mattered now anyway. He knew what he'd find there.

In the early morning the village seemed to be stirring on the very edge of wakefulness, as if in a moment the milkman would come rattling through the silent streets in his electric cart, the postman on his pushbike, the paperboy, the people going to work. The man stood on the motorway and looked down on the sleeping houses, the dreaming streets and wondered if perhaps this time it might be different.

The motorway here ran across a bridge spanning a narrow point of a little downward fold in the misty vale. The village nestled comfortably in the fold, clustering about a little river, so quiet and still that it seemed to hold the promise of life as he stood on the bridge and leaned on the rail and looked down at the houses, just being touched by the dawn sun. The man flipped a mental coin.

The slope down to the village was steep, grassy and dew-sparkled, and he slipped and fell twice, the second time sliding to the bottom of the slope and staggering ankle-deep into the shallows of the river where it whispered beneath the motorway. He found a path which ran beside the river and followed it until it reached the village.

The first house he tried was locked up. The front door of the next stood partly open. He pushed it wide open and stood in the doorway. The door opened straight into the kitchen, and the air inside smelled rich and musty. Not rotten, as it did sometimes when he went into a house. Just musty. Mouldy. The damp must have got in, with the door open like that.

The segs in his boots clicked on the flags as he stepped across the kitchen, tried the taps. The cold had been turned off and the hot had been left on, and the tank had run out. He found the stopcock under the sink and turned it on, but still no water came out. The refrigerator was full of rotten food. A clammy breath of foul air gusted into his face when he opened the door. Meat had gone bad, vegetables and fruit had gone sick and runny. Something awful had happened to three bottles of milk. The breadbin was full of blue and green mould.

In the hall the carpet was wet and squishy underfoot; the stair carpet, gone mouldy, seemed to have begun to grow of its own volition, like some surreal form of life. The damp had got in. That door . . .

No money, or valuables of any kind, were to be found in the house. Useful items like knives, guns and shells, clothes, tools, were likewise missing. It seemed the occupants had lived long enough to get out with their possessions.

Outside in the fresh air again, he wandered slowly up the street, trying doors and windows as he went. Down here in the village everything seemed cooler, darker than up on the motorway. The sun, rising behind the bridge, cast great shadows on the buildings. He felt as if he had somehow, without knowing it, stepped down into some other world, a cold, empty, sleeping world, parallel to but entirely separate from the world above, outside this tiny little crease in the ground. Everything here was hard and sharp. Cold and dead.

Further down the street he found another house with its door open. As he put the flat of his hand against the door he caught that sicksweet rotting smell. It gathered, jagged at the back of his nose, stung on his sinuses and caught on his palate, like a warning. He stopped in the motion of pushing open the door, eyes stung by the smell. Then he stepped back, took his hand from the wood, and walked up the path to the garden gate.

In the middle of the village, like a heart, stood the post office, a one-storey whitewashed building with red window frames, the bottom half of the windows blued out and Savings Bank stickers in them. The door was locked, and it didn't look as if anyone had been inside for a long time. He walked round the building once.

Outside the post office stood a skeleton gateway of square-section metal tubing, a little more than man-high and about two men wide. Attached to one of the uprights at chest height was a square push-button telephone dial, and lower down at the side, a metal box.

He walked up to the gate and pushed down on the lid of the box. The directory came up easily, flapped open where pages had been torn out. The covers were time-chewed and scribbled-on, and no page had escaped some pen or other. He pursed his lips and let the book fall shut again. One of the curled covers caught between the book and the edge of the box, and the directory jammed half closed. He left it.

You could dial anywhere in Britain with six digits, always assuming the power was still on. A gate didn't need very much power, but it couldn't run on nothing. He punched six random numbers, waited for the little light to go on, and flicked a twig through the gate.

It vanished without a flicker.

The little light went out, and suddenly the magic was gone again. The gate was once more just a metal structure, as dead as the rest of the structures in the village. He could call the magic back again; the spell only lasted six digits, but it wasn't worth it. He noted the gate's number in his notebook, and the village's name, then continued up the street.

At the top of the street there was a large open green, bordered on one side by a little stagnant, duckless duckpond. In the centre of the green there was a great pile of earth, still damp from the mist and dew, about three times his height and as long as two buses parked end-to-end, like one of the old Norse barrows. The grass about its base was scorched and blackened, as if the earth had been piled on top of the site of some great bonfire. He stepped onto the dew-sparkling grass and walked across the green to the foot of the barrow, hands in pockets. It must have been here quite a while, for scrappy tufts of grass and moss dotted its face. At one end there was a paving slab, leaned up against the slope. On it were scratched the faint words

HERE WE BURNED THE BODIES OF 583 MEN, WOMEN
AND CHILDREN,
LAST SURVIVORS OF THE VILLAGE OF LAYTON FORD.
WE WEPT.

Back on the bridge the sun was gaining strength, a warm yellow coin risen now above the slowly dispersing mist. The morning was still and warm, a prophecy of a scorcher of a day. He looked away from the village and south. The motorway laid a solid grey ribbon through rough green. Fields, unharvested, continued their slow march to overwhelm the great concrete artifact. Seeds, falling in cracks in the roadway, had germinated, in some places cracking and breaking the concrete. It was like some great organism, slowly rejecting a foreign body.

He was quite sure now that there was nobody else along this stretch of motorway. He carefully cross-hatched lines on the map along the red line of the motorway, folded the map and looked about him. Another empty village. Another open gate, so to speak. At least there was a power station still working somewhere, with the logical inference that there was someone still running it. He couldn't recall how many people it took to crew a power station, but he knew it must be quite a few. All the gates along this motor-way were still working, suggesting that perhaps more than one power station was still working. And he hadn't seen a living soul since starting out.

After the village the motorway ran away through a notch cut in the steep face of the Downs. Shouldering his rucksack, he walked away from the village and on towards the little notch in the hills.

He reached the gap around noon, when the sun had whitened overhead and burned the mist out of the valley and struck shivering waves of air up from the surface of the motorway in front and behind him. He stopped in the cutting and looked back along the motorway and across the valley at the crest he had come over that morning. He couldn't see the village among the trees, but every-thing looked very small and still and perfect, like the accessories to some toy train layout.

Before him, infinite and indistinct in the heat-haze, the Downs rolled away under bright sun, buzzing with the heat. He was sweat-ing now from the long jog up the gentle slope out of the valley to the cutting, and had taken off his jacket and unbuttoned his shirt to the waist.

Far, far away, beyond a point where the heat-haze made Downs and sky become one, was a bright line of silver light, infinitely thin. The haze made the motorway fade towards the line of the sunlit sea, as if it was entering another universe. It was still a very, very long way off. The sun made him squint, and he put on his sun-glasses again before moving on.

He had been walking for an hour or so before he realised why the valley had seemed like a toy. Perfect, still, sleeping detail.

No people . . .

Roy Preston had stumbled on transplacement as a theoretical possibility while working on the structure of elementary particles. It was one of those strange scientific sidesteps that only happen very rarely, and Preston, though never doubting the validity of his theory, could never understand why it worked at all. In many ways, it might have been better if Preston had died out there in Scotland, or missed the theory, or perhaps if he'd never been born at all. As it was, he built a prototype transplacement generator, convinced NASA to help him develop it, and lived to see the consequences.

A breeze picked up as he walked down the centre of the middle southbound lane. It flapped his shirt and cooled the sweat on his body. About half a mile down the motorway, in the northbound lanes, was a knot of metal, disrupting the smooth sweep of concrete. Coming up level with it, he saw it was a pile-up of something like twenty cars, torn and buckled and rusting, blocking all three lanes. Behind it, a scatter of cars had been abandoned, their way blocked by the pile-up. He noted that all their tyres had gone, and the bonnets of most stood open where the engines had been removed. No doubt their tanks had been emptied too. A long time ago. They were rusting, sitting on the concrete on their wheelrims, strange crumbling structures in metal and glass and plastic, memorials to the civilisation they represented.

He was surprised to find any cars at all. Transplacement hadn't made the motor car extinct, but most people had sold their cars, himself included, as a gate was infinitely cheaper. It had never occurred to him that some people might not want to get rid of their car.

The breeze blew the smell of the Downs across his path, the scent of forests far away, of lakes and rivers, the heady smell of freshly-mown grass, of crops gone wild for ages now, of . . . freshly-mown grass, and . . . smoke . . .

The pub was tucked away in a stand of tall trees, a great rambling half-timber building, its windows hundreds of diamond-shaped sections of glass trapped in matrices of lead, its chimney gently breathing a subliminal wisp of grey smoke The little bit of lawn in front of the building was newly-mown; a lawnmower stood under a tree beside a pile of fresh, damp clippings.

The door was open, and he stepped slowly into the rich, beery dimness of the bar. Inside everything was undisturbed, neat and tidy. The bottles on the shelves were arranged, labels facing outward, the pumps uncovered and dully gleaming with polish, the glasses behind the bar clear and sparkling, the tables clean and polished, chairs arranged, bar counter clean, a cloth folded beside the pumps. The bar was empty, but like the village its very perfection, its stillness, seemed to hold promise of life.

He took off his sunglasses, put the rucksack down in the open doorway and walked up to the bar, touched the folded cloth. It was still damp, and there were faintly damp streaks on the counter. He looked up, and through the open door he could just see the motorway, and the indistinct lumpy shape of the pile-up against the sky. He shuddered a little at how close he had come to walking right on by.

"Can I help you, sir?"

He turned. She was small, twisted about herself. Golden hair hung down her back, failed to camouflage the ruined shoulder, failed to hide the scars where it fell across her face. The blue denim dress bulged in all the wrong places, making her shape against the open back door seem alien. In one hand she held a faded rag doll, all floppy.

Again, "Can I help you, sir?"

Not used to speaking to people, he hesitated a moment. "Er, have you any beer?" and a moment later it struck him how ridiculous the words sounded. His voice sounded false and forced.

Her left leg dragged as she limped round behind the counter, lowered the flap. "Only bottles of lager, I'm afraid. Deliveries have fallen off just lately."

Unsure whether that was sarcasm or not, or even if he could still recognise sarcasm when he heard it, he shrugged. "That'll be fine. I haven't any money, though."

She smiled lopsidedly as she took a frosty bottle from the fridge. "That's all right. We accept credit cards."

"Oh," he said, still not sure whether she was serious or not.

There was a tired sigh from the doorway. "Margaret . . ."

Pouring the beer, she looked up. "We've got a customer,

Tommy," she said. "I told him we only have bottles of lager, but he says he doesn't mind."

He was tall, but one hip was an odd, crushed shape, and his left arm ended at the elbow. He had long sandy hair and a scrappy beard and moustache. He limped up to the counter, leaned over, took the bottle from her and stood it on the counter. "Margaret, I've told you before not to play with the bottles." He looked round. "Sorry; I'm not sure if this stuff is fit to drink any more. It's been here ages now."

He shrugged. "The whisky ought to be okay."

Tommy smiled. "Sure." He lifted the flap and walked round the counter, took an unopened bottle and two glasses and carried them over to a table. He sat down with difficulty, the stiff hip obviously giving him pain, and then relaxed back in his chair, breathing hard. "Please, sit down, Mr . . ."

Something silly made him say, "Palmer. Ray Palmer."

Tommy waved the stump of his left arm. "Mr Palmer."

He sat down opposite Tommy, broke the seal on the bottle and poured two hefty measures of Scotch. It all seemed horribly unreal, distant, like a dream. He handed one glass to Tommy, who sipped slowly, savouring the drink. "I must apologise for Margaret, Mr Palmer," he said at length.

He dismissed it with a shrug. "Kids will be kids."

Tommy gave a faint, sad smile. "She's my wife."

He looked round, watched her limp slowly out into the sunshine, the floppy rag doll in her hand. "Oh, I'm sorry—"

Tommy shook his head and looked at his drink.

There was an uncomfortable silence, then he said, "What happened?"

Tommy didn't look up from his drink. "We were in an accident four years ago." He nodded at the open front door. "You can see it from here."

He felt a tiny electric jump in his stomach. "You were in that?"

Tommy grunted. "Strange to be living within sight of it, I suppose, but we're at peace here. Margaret got the worst of it. She's thirty-two and she's got the mind of a seven-year-old, Mr Palmer." And he lifted his eyes. Cold, empty, crippled eyes. He looked away, veiling the pain. "I cut myself sharpening the blades of the lawn-mower two years ago. Gangrene."

He frowned. "Who amputated then?"

Tommy jerked his head. "There's a commune about four miles away. They've got a doctor, cottage hospital, forge, about seven hundred folk in all." He sipped his Scotch again. "They're why Margaret's still alive and I can still walk, after a fashion. All the others died. Fifty-two people. Men, women, kids. I buried them on the other side of the motorway."

"I was told there was nobody alive south of London."

"Where have you come from?"

"Stoke. You're the first people I've met since I started. Everywhere else is dead."

Tommy smiled faintly. "We thought there was nobody alive north of London. Some people in the Scottish Highlands, perhaps, but not many." He sat back. "It's amazing the way people hang on to life. I thought Margaret was going to die after the accident. Sometimes I wish she had." He rubbed his eyes. "And God help me for saying that."

The question burned its way to the surface at last. "Why were you all driving cars?"

Tommy looked him in the eye. "Nobody trusted the gates."

He felt a hot wave of guilt flood him. "Oh, yeah."

First there had been slight psychological effects; jumping across datelines caused gatelag. To a generation inured to jetlag, it seemed a problem they could get used to. Others experienced slight transplacement disorientation when they stepped from one place to another. It didn't seem all that common, so transplacement shock remained a minor effect for a while.

It only became a serious problem about two years after gates came into use. The number of people suffering from transplacement shock was growing steadily, and the attacks were becoming more and more serious. People were found wandering the streets, unsure of where they were or where they had come from. Some of the cases looked permanent, and by the time anyone worked out what was going wrong it was already too late. Hundreds of cases were being found each week.

The human mind, used to millions of years of slower travel, couldn't stand being whipped instantaneously from one place to another, couldn't grasp the displacement from one place to another without a space between, refused to accept it, and became hopelessly lost trying to place itself. The effect didn't seem so bad if you had a firm, clear idea of where you were going, but most people just dialled and stepped through the gate. And became . . . lost.

Gates mysteriously ceased to function. The weather affected outside installations and made them do strange things; the engineers were always just a step behind. In Britain alone just under six hundred people had stepped into gates and not come out anywhere. The Government hadn't told anyone about them; by then it had other gate problems.

The World Health Organisation had tried to delay the introduction of gates several times at the United Nations, and each time it had been overruled. The advantages outweighed the disadvantages, so long as people were careful. People weren't careful, as usual. Transplacement could spread typhoid from Calcutta to Croydon in the time it took to dial four digits, then up to half a dozen more, then step through . . .

If transplacement had come three years later, perhaps immunology would have been ready for it; as it was, plagues started in one place, then erupted in another, perhaps a thousand miles away. It was impossible to stop once it had begun. Soon there weren't enough people to try . . .

"Where are you going, Mr Palmer?" asked Tommy.

"I'm going to try to get to the Isle of Wight. They never installed gates, and word is, they were almost untouched by the plagues."

Margaret came up behind him. "You said your name's Mr Palmer?"

He poured himself some more Scotch. "That's right, Margaret."

"Then why does it say your name's Mr Preston on your bag?"

He forced himself to look round slowly at the rucksack, still standing in the doorway. He'd forgotten all about it.

"Margaret," said Tommy. "Now you apologise to Mr Palmer."

Surprised how calm he felt, he said, "It's okay, Tommy. It isn't my bag, Margaret. It belonged to a friend of mine. His name was Preston." He wasn't surprised how easily the lie came to him.

"Is he dead?" she asked.

Tommy closed his eyes and sighed.

He smiled gently. "Yes, he's dead now." Which in a way, he supposed, was true. He stood up. "Well, I'd better get on. I've a long way to go still."

Tommy stood with him. "Of course. Is there anything you need?"

"No, thank you."

Margaret said, "Has he paid for his drink, Tommy?"

Back on the motorway, he stood by the piled-up cars and looked across at the field on the other side. He counted the fifty-two mounds, all grassed over now, some indistinct under the green. All dead in a motor accident in the age of instant travel, and Tommy and Margaret in their pub. All because nobody trusted the gates. And the rest of the world dead because they *had* trusted them.

In the end, he thought, whose fault is it all?

He'd long since found it wasn't that simple, and perhaps he'd found an answer of sorts in that.

Preston picked up his rucksack and slung it over one shoulder and set off down the motorway in search of Paradise. Walking all the way . . .

And Duncans Horses,
(A thing most strange and certaine)
Beauteous, and swift, the minions of their Race,
Turned wilde in nature, broke their stalls, flong out,
Contending 'gainst Obedience, as they would
Make Warre with Mankinde.

Macbeth, II. iv.

how to
save the world
and influence people

In many cases, sound defines location. So: the soft whisper of waves
on a long shore, the sea murmuring idiot against the sand, a silent
breeze softly sighing in over the emptiness and finally rising on the
scarred face of some frowning white cliff . . .

Eyes shut, he turned over slowly in the shallow wetness, tasted
brackish water on his lips. Fresh water. Light dappled on his closed
lids. Fresh water.

In many cases, sound defines location. Other things modify the
definition. Taste, for instance. Fresh water . . .

On his back, he forced his eyes open against the dim light. Trees
dissected blue sky, silhouetted leaves whispering nonsense sea-
sounds to each other in the soft breeze. Painfully slowly, he turned
over in the shallow pool and lay on his stomach, supporting himself
on his forearms, watching ripples slide smoothly away to rock the
weeds on the edge of the pool. Something tiny and quick brushed
his knuckles.

The little pool was almost circular, ringed with sentinel trees and
fed by a little chuckling brook, pebble-bedded. Beyond the trees
everything faded away in indistinct dimness. Away somewhere in
the musty dim light a wood pigeon clattered among the trees, clap-
ping dull echoes out of the silent wood.

Another definition, modified by sight: a morning in the woods.

Other definitions didn't come. Identity, for instance. Frowning, he crawled across the pool and lay in the sodden vegetation at the edge, eyes closed again, trying to catch on some foggy scrap of recall; anything at all to serve as an anchor, but there was nothing to hang on to, nothing to define his position in time or events. He didn't know where he was, and he didn't know who he was. Lost, in the worst kind of way.

He lay in the shallows for a long time, half his face in the water, before stirring slowly and hauling himself to his knees, dripping and cold, in the mud and wet grass, everything still and quiet as a caught breath. He stood up slowly and squelched out through the mud onto the firmer ground beyond, where he fell exhausted on the short, dew-sparkled turf and fainted from the effort.

There was no way of telling how much later it was when he came to himself again. A long time perhaps; perhaps not. He was still wet, still felt tired and sick. He got to his knees and stood slowly from there, stumbled a few steps to lean against a tree. The effort made him feel light-headed and nauseous, but he fought it down and managed to stumble another few steps to the next tree, where he rested before he moved on again.

In this way he managed to totter almost forty yards from the pool before the nausea overcame him, and leaning against a tree he vomited a dark, bitter liquid that burned throat and palate, making his eyes water. The spasms made his chest hurt.

When it was finished he stumbled weakly from tree to tree, directionless and without caring. Somewhere, like a subliminal echo from the far side of a mountain, the faint smell of things burning stained the air, mingling itself with the forest smells.

The trees were thinning now, the gaps between them more difficult to negotiate without falling over, and he had to resort to stumbling headlong just to reach the next tree.

Eventually, tired and sick, he reached the edge of the woodland and leaned against a tree breathing heavily, and looked down the bare hillside into the valley. Far below, hedges and walls demarcated fields, trees were dark spots clumped among rich crops, stone farmhouses grey structures almost lost in the fields. Far, far away, almost on the horizon, he could just make out the dark vague bulk of the other side of the valley, a little lower than the hillside he stood on.

Looking back along the valley he saw a great pall of smoke, a cancer smudged onto the bright clear day.

Away down the valley, a city was on fire.

*

The narrowboat's engine chugged softly into silence as she entered the lock. Forward, Charlie and his son swarmed up the ladder in the lock wall to help Maureen close the gates. Roger leaned on the tiller and brushed raindrops from his fringe. Behind him the gates swung slowly shut, and Charlie went across the top to the controls on the other side. A moment later there was the sound of surging water over the pattering rain, and the boat started to rise.

Jan poked her head up out of the midships hatch, hair sleep-tousled, nose wrinkled against the rain. She looked at him, mouthed, Okay? under the roar of the water. He nodded, and she went back inside.

The top of the lock fell slowly towards him, and the edge withdrew below his eye level, revealing a small grassy space beyond the towpath, and beyond that a little white and black cottage, door open, chimney whispering smoke. A young girl stood in the doorway, watching them. On the other side of the canal a wood drifted misty in the rain. Hidden somewhere, a dog barked.

Jan came up out of the aft hatch and stood beside him in Arran sweater, jeans through at the knee, feet bare. "Where are we?" she asked, brushing hair away from her face.

"Ayton lock," he said, watching the water level slowly rise. "We'll be there by dinner time."

"In plenty of time not to perform," she said, glowering up at the clouds.

"It'll stop," he said. "It's only a shower."

"You said that last time, and it rained for three days."

He smiled. "I can't be right all the time."

"Not even some of the time?" She grinned and started to go

89

back down the hatch, stopped, looked up at the sky, and shouted, "Stop raining!"

He made a face. "Jan."

She smiled at him and shrugged, and went back inside.

A moment later the thunder of the sluices stopped, and the water in the lock became still again. Maureen and Gary jumped aboard, and Charlie and the lock keeper opened the gates. Roger started up the engine and guided the boat out into the canal beyond. Charlie stayed a moment longer with the keeper, then jogged along the towpath and got on board. Roger steered the boat away from the bank, and they were off again.

"No sweat," said Charlie, puffing on his pipe and leaning back against the hatchway coaming. He smiled and looked about him. "It's even stopped raining, look."

Roger sighed and pulled back the hood of his kagool. "So it has."

Sometimes they did little vignettes of the history of the canals, sometimes they did Shakespeare, sometimes they just did songs. Charlie liked to think they were the only troupe of wandering minstrels on the canals, at least with such a varied repertoire. He liked the idea of travelling on the narrowboat, and he and his family had been with her for six years now, wandering the waterways. Sometimes it got out of hand. He'd once tried to buy a great Shire to tow the boat, even though it had a perfectly functional diesel engine. They'd had to outvote him quickly.

Tonight it was songs. Roger liked doing songs; he couldn't remember the lines when they did plays, and he felt silly doing the canal stories sometimes, as Charlie had adapted them from traditional stories and he tended to inject a liberal amount of farce into them.

Charlie was on the tiller when they arrived in the grounds of Endean House. The canal cut a great curved swathe through tamed woods and manicured parkland, and they moored the boat beside where some chairs had been set up on the bank. Charlie went up to the house while the others had dinner, and afterwards they unpacked all the gear and put it on the bank.

They set the amps out first; four little battery practice amps that Charlie had bought from someone in Stoke. Speakers arranged . . . so. Mikes, stands. They sat Maureen in various seats to make sure that everyone would be able to hear properly.

"It'd be better if you were in tune," she said.

"I'm in tune," Jan said, twirling her flute like a cheerleader's baton.

Roger unplugged his bass. "You're flat."

"I am not," she said, indignant. "He's sharp." Jerking her head in Gary's direction.

Gary tucked his plectrum between the strings. "What a load of nonsense," he murmured.

Maureen sighed. "Come on, kiddies, everybody in the right key for mummy."

Jan put her flute down beside the mikestand. "Heads up," she said quietly. "Looks like thunder."

Charlie strode wrathfully across the grass, flat cap pushed back, waistcoat undone. He vented a growl and sat down heavily in the back row with his arms crossed.

"How many guesses do we get?" Jan called.

Charlie sighed and waved a hand vaguely. "You'd better start packing everything away. The show's been cancelled."

Maureen made a face. "Did they say why?"

He shrugged. "They've had some sort of 'bad trouble' and the people don't want to come out after dusk." He took his cap off. "I said we could reschedule the show, but he said don't bother."

"You're kidding," said Jan.

"That's what he told me. Something about ghosts and witches and little green men. One or two kiddies have gone missing and some of the village people have seen . . . 'things' abroad in the evenings."

Jan and Roger exchanged glances. Roger said, "That's silly."

He nodded. "And I bloody well told him so too, for all the good it did me." He heaved a great sigh. "By, there's nowt so odd as folk."

Maureen smiled. "We've got the advance money, though."

He nodded. "Aye. We can tie up here tonight and move on tomorrow. You all deserve a bit of a rest."

Roger put his bass back in its case, shut the lid. "How far is the village from here?"

Charlie shrugged. "Mile, mile and a half. Why?"

Roger looked at Jan, then back at Charlie. "We thought we'd take a bit of a walk."

"Aren't you scared of the ghosts and witches and little green men?"

Jan laughed.

Roger said, "Of course not. It's not dark yet."

In Endean they traded pints in the local pub, wandered hand in hand through the village, window-shopping. It all looked normal enough; a busy, bustling little village on market day. But it felt wrong, in a horribly nameless way. It felt terribly, terribly wrong.

Coming out of the market, Jan stopped and nudged him, jerked her chin towards the buildings across the street.

He looked up. Across the street the paint on the window frames of some of the houses was charred and blistered, as if by great heat, while on the other houses it was still untouched. Under the affected windows the brick had faded in long uneven pale bands.

He looked at her. "Well?"

She jerked her head backward. "The blistered window frames coincide with the gaps in the row of houses opposite. The unaffected areas are in the shadow of the houses opposite. It's like something had been . . . I don't know. It's as if something was shone on the town, something that blistered the paint."

"Radiation?"

She shrugged. "Whatever it was, it was low down; below the rooftops. And it was behind us."

It took him a moment to get his bearings. "That's back towards the canal."

She nodded. "Yeah."

*

They came to him in the night, raging like flames into his head. Lost, crying, weeping kitten-voices plaintive screaming. They were looking for him looking for him singling him out by process of elimination looking looking and they'd found . . . found . . . a ring of fire burning dancing crying in his soul crying crying crying.

Jan put her arms round him, held him to her. "Rog—"

"Oh, there's a burning in my head, Jan, I can hear it thunder. Hydrogen fusion; can you smell the smoke? It's coming from my ears now, streams of it light years long. Oh God God there's barbed wire in my mouth, I'm speaking barbs and they're crying to me."

She shook him gently. "Tell them to go away, Rog," she whispered.

He opened his eyes. "Barbed wire," he breathed. "It cuts . . ."

"I know," she said.

"They've found me, Jan. They've found me and even I don't know who I am."

"It's all right, Rog." She rolled away from him. "Go away, cloud."

He sighed. "Do you suppose they know who I am, Jan?"

"Perhaps. I don't know."

He was calmer now the fit was subsiding. "Jan."

"Yes?" Moonlight spilled through the window, silver across their legs as the clouds revealed the moon.

"When you found me, why did you call me Roger?"

She smiled. "First name that came into my head."

"Why are you here?"

The smile went slowly away. "Perhaps you'll find out soon."

(When he woke again later the moon bobbed its face in and out of drifting cloud. Head against his shoulder, Jan breathed slowly, eyes shut. Across the canal a wood breasted a low hill, made a ragged silhouette against the moon-illumined cloudbank. Frost sparkled on the other bank, scattered diamond dust, a crystal environment just beyond the glass. On this side everything warm and

93

cosy, on the other everything cold and sharp. He put his arm round her shoulder, gently kissed the top of her head. For the first time in a long while, he felt he belonged somewhere.)

(The moon had submerged a little further when he opened his eyes again; the top of the wood cut an uneven cord out of its underside. He could see its light flooding between the trees on top of the hill. Everything still and crisp. Fragile. Under one of the trees, black against the moon's silver backlight, stood a tall emaciated stick-figure. Easily fifteen feet high it stood, and matchstick thin, and its head was lost amongst the lower foliage, though its long hair could be descried, blowing, blowing bannerlike in the breeze. Its arms, stick-thin, reached down to its knees, and in one gaunt knob of a fist it held one end of something long and thin and hard, like a sword. He lay beside Jan, examining the scene. From the cant of its body, the figure might have been looking down on the narrowboat, but it was hard to tell. Somehow, the shape was a familiar thing, and like most familiar things it held no terror. When next he looked, it had fled back into the realm of night and dream.)

*

"I've decided to stay on another season," he said over breakfast.

"You can't act," Gary commented, tucking into a bowl of milk-soggy cornflakes.

Maureen tapped him in reproof. "Give over, Gary. I thought you said—"

He nodded. "Yeah, I know. I know. I've finally made a definite decision, though. I like it here."

Charlie sat back chewing on a piece of toast and hooked a thumb through one of his braces. "It was always an open-ended thing, Roger. You're welcome to stay on after this run if you want to."

Under the table, Jan took his hand in hers. "I'd like to stay on too, Charlie. If you can spare the room."

Maureen grinned. "Yes, you two do seem to go together, don't you?"

Charlie's bushy brows approached each other in deep thought. "A Permanent Floating Minstrel Troupe," he mused. Then he too grinned. "We don't ever need to break a run; just keep on going."

"Like the Flying Dutchman," Gary said quietly to his breakfast. Charlie nodded to himself. "Aye, it's a bloody good idea too." He gestured with his toast, shook crumbs everywhere. "I'll cut you in on the Troupe. A quarter of everything."

Gary looked up. "A fifth, don't you mean?"

Charlie nodded. "Aye, when you get old enough. Well, Roger?"

Jan smiled and squeezed his hand, and he nodded. "It's a great idea, Charlie."

Jan brought coffee to the tiller, steaming in a big art-design mug, and stood with him as the narrowboat chugged gently along the canal.

"You may not realise it, but that was a very significant decision," she said, nestling into her thick blue trenchcoat.

He cupped the mug in his hands, absorbing the warmth. "Oh yes?"

"It's the first decision you've made entirely on your own, for yourself, since I found you in my garden. Do you know what that means?"

Something large and grey moved slowly in the trees on the starboard bank of the canal. He prided himself on being able to tell port from starboard. Jan always got them mixed. "I have a feeling you're going to tell me anyway, whether I know or not."

She smiled. "It means your personality's stable and you've learned to trust it."

The grey thing, which had vanished for a moment behind clumps of holly, appeared again. It had four legs and a long, thick neck. He could see silver flash dully, hear the faint tinkle of tiny bells.

"Suddenly you're my psychiatrist," he said, adjusting the tiller slightly.

She yawned. "No, I mean it. Remember how you used to talk all the time about wondering who you really were? How you sat in front of the fire back home and told me how scared you were that you might be a murderer or something? You don't do that any more; you don't care any more."

He frowned. "I still don't know how it happened. That bothers me sometimes."

"Yes, but it's not a vital part of you any more."

"Maybe not," he said.

It was on the towpath now: a great grey Percheron in black leather tack, silver bells on bridle and pommel. It had to step carefully because of the narrowness of the path. Its rider was huge and skeletal; he wore a black cloak, and a great longsword was girt at his waist.

"When you lay down to die in my garden that night, you were nobody. Nothing. Just an empty thing, not even clothed. All the time since I found you, since we joined the boat, it's all made you what you are now."

"So what am I?"

"You're Roger. Roger who is part of a *Permanent* Floating Minstrel Troupe." She kissed him. "And Jan loves him."

Across the canal, the towpath reared up in a single brick span. The Percheron reached the bridge first, stood waiting at the crest.

Jan looked at it. "The way I see it," she said, "we have two choices. We might just keep going under the bridge, or we might stop and finally find out what they want."

He smiled. "No contest." And he reached forward and turned off the engine.

Tall he sat in the saddle, tall and gaunt. Between the laces of his waistcoat, ribs sharply scored dark, tanned skin. His face was a barely-fleshed skull, just fleshy enough to erase the skull's natural grin. His eyes glowed from far back in gaunt, bony pits.

"Do you know me?" The voice was quiet, but so was everything else, suddenly. No wind, no birds . . .

Fascinated, Roger watched the almost naked larynx bob and dance in the thin ribbing of the throat cartilages, and something stirred deep within him, where he had thought there was nothing. "I recognise you," he said haltingly. "I think . . ."

"Then you know my purpose."

He stood frowning, trying to catch onto the foggy scrap of recall, to use it as an anchor, but upon examination, he found it not to be there at all, like the echo of an illusion.

"I don't . . . what . . . what do you want?"

The smouldering red eyes regarded him like glowing cinders in deep wells. "I know who you are." Behind the great horse, three silver-suited figures moved into sight and stood at the parapet looking down at them. They wore bulbous white helmets with dark visors, and bulky white backpacks. The contrast between the tall thing on the horse and the obvious artificiality of the other three figures' suits was so sudden and marked that he managed to tear his eyes from the glowing rednesses in that head. He heard Jan take a long breath.

"You're Death," he said. "My world's death." And in naming, some of the terror came and blossomed within him.

A bare grin, pared right down to nothing. "My world." Turn of the head, nod. "And their world."

Jan said, "Cadence."

Water frothed, the small cruel head darted, water ran on the neck, black eyes caught the sun; deep down in the canal something rumbled, and the dragon spat fire, washed white opaque heat across the bridge, wiped out, blotted everything standing there. There was an awful smell of living things burning, brick charring, cracking.

When it was over and Jan was leaning over the edge of the boat and patting the dragon's head, Roger said, "Too easy."

She straightened up, and the slick head slipped back beneath the surface. "Yes, it always is," she said, a little sadly. "They're sitting ducks."

He took a long slow breath. "Are you going to tell me now?"

She turned, and those fathomless green eyes fixed him for a moment before turning away, veiled. "The Exodus has been going on for six thousand years now. I don't know where they come from, and I'm not certain how they get here, but every year two or three arrive, and most years we get them. All I'm really sure about is that if enough of them get here, they'll take Earth."

"We."

She nodded. "For some reason, they only appear in Britain and China. There's about a thousand of us scattered around in Britain and China, around the most likely appearance loci. We've been doing it for a long long time now. My mother, and hers before her. We try to keep it in the family, sort of."

"With the dragons."

She nodded. "Or cats, if we feel like being subtle. Cats can sense when they're near."

He looked up at the charred, smoking brickwork. "What was the . . . other thing? Was it Death?" And the moment he said it, he knew that was silly. How could they kill Death?

Her forehead creased and her mouth tightened. "That . . . that was something very old. Something they corrupted to their needs." She shuddered a little. "I'm glad it's gone."

He rubbed his eyes. "We still don't know what they wanted me for."

She shook her head. "And we never will now. Hardly matters now, does it? If it had mattered to you, you'd have asked it. Wouldn't you?"

He looked down at the gently roiled surface of the canal. "You can't stop an invasion."

"We've done all right so far."

"There'll be more."

She nodded gently. "We'll get them, though."

He shook his head. "It's hopeless, Jan."

She smiled and took his hand as she went inside to wake up Charlie and his family. "It's a start, Rog. It's a start."

*

He'd been a long time getting here. At first he could only move short distances before fatigue overwhelmed him, but slowly he seemed to gain strength as he drew nearer to the city, burning, fuming on the bright day, as if it was feeding him. The skin had been stripped from the soles of his feet by sharp stones, and there were crimson prints of his feet glistening on the road behind him.

Somewhere in the long, straight river far away across the valley, perhaps a long gaily-painted narrowboat chugged on forever with a dragon breasting its wake, searching for things which might not have been there at all.

Something small and silver-clad lay heaped in the middle of the road, headless on the edge of a dark pool of something glistening dry. Not far away there was rumour and disturbance, but the city blotted all.

The first houses were not burned, nor the first large tower blocks, windows empty-eyed. The fire was in the city's heart, eating out from within like a decay. On a black wall someone had written QUO VADIS? in great sprawling yellow chalk letters. More war. Why then Ile fit you. Mad againe.

He stopped, and even before he noticed the nail wounds through his wrists he knew he was on a loser again.

[I've got] fairies at the bottom of my garden

Wednesday

Halford was early down to breakfast that morning, otherwise he'd have missed it. There was no earthly reason why he shouldn't have slept in like he did every morning, but this particular morning he clambered out of bed, unable to sleep, glowered at himself in the bathroom mirror, and stumbled downstairs into the kitchen.

Two slices of bread toasting under the grill and the kettle bubbling, he leaned on the draining board and looked out of the window. There had been rain, but just a light shower, enough to swell the dewdrops on the roses and the silver specks on the lawn, and make the dying, browning conifer at the bottom of the garden look awfully droopy and forlorn. He pursed his lips and frowned at the dying tree, almost hidden in a corner of the garden. He didn't know why it was dying, or what to do to save it. He'd invested in a conifer book, but it hadn't helped much, so he'd finally had to resign himself to the fact that the tree was going to die. It looked a pretty nasty way for a tree to go.

The kettle was boiling. He turned off the switch, unplugged the kettle and poured the water into the teapot. He was carrying the pot over to the side when he smelled bread burning, and a thread of smoke twirled up from the cooker. He turned, and boiling tea slopped out of the pot and splashed onto his bare right foot. He shouted, and the pot slipped from his hands and smashed in a crash of pot and tea on the tiled floor. He danced away from the boiling splash, whipped the toast out from under the grill and tipped it into the sink, two slices of smoking charcoal. Halford sat down in a chair and yelled a swearword. Breakfast was a disaster.

Later, standing with a slice of bread and marmalade and a tin of stout, Halford looked out and saw Pan coming up the path with something in his mouth, his face all masked with red. He scowled. All he needed right now was blood all over the kitchen. He toyed briefly with the idea of blocking Pan's little door with a stool, but the cat was too quick for him, and all glossy black and sweeping tail he darted through, lord of all he surveyed, and looked about the kitchen to satisfy himself that his domain hadn't been altered in his absence. The jewel green eyes fell on Halford and regarded him steadily.

"Do you have to make such a mess?" said Halford.

Of course, said the eyes. I'm a cat. I'm supposed to kill little furry things.

Only it wasn't a little furry thing. It was a lump of blood and gore the size of a quite substantial rat, and the cat was having difficulty carrying it. Bits of cloth were plastered to the gore, and long strands of golden hair, and strange jewelled flashes like the colour on a butterfly's wing. Whatever it was, it most certainly wasn't a little furry thing.

Halford put aside plate and beer, and bent down. The cat backed away a little, the eyes appealing, What do you want it for?

He put out a hand. "Come on; I won't eat it. I just want to look at it, that's all."

Distrustfully (you can live with a cat, but somehow you never get the impression that it completely trusts you) Pan released the bloody thing into Halford's hand. Still warm, it was disgusting to touch, and so slippery-bloody that it slipped from his hand and smacked wetly on the tiles. His stomach did a queasy thing, and he had to force himself to touch it again, to hold the tiny scraps of bloody cloth between the tips of his fingers and pull them aside, but the thing was so desperately mangled that it was impossible to tell what it might have been. He turned it over slowly with a poking forefinger, and something bright and golden flashed embedded in the bloody flesh. He gently, carefully teased it out, and all of a sudden his stomach felt cold and hard. The bright golden thing was attached to a tiny scrap of leather.

It was a tiny shoe, with a golden buckle.

After he'd cleaned up the mess Halford sat at the kitchen table and stared at the little shoe, several equally ridiculous things running through his mind at the same time. Under his magnifying glass the shoe was revealed to be of perfect workmanship and proportion. He could see the minute stitching which bound the upper to the sole, and an even finer line of stitching which made patterns on the band that ran across the shoe and through the buckle. There were even faint scuff marks on the toe. And that scared him most of all.

He sat back with his big mug of steaming tea, finally made without mishap, and looked at the shoe with its tiny, perfectly cast golden buckle. It gleamed in the early morning sunlight that gushed in through the window.

It couldn't possibly be a real shoe, to fit a real foot. The man whose foot fitted that shoe would have to be under a foot high; seven or eight inches at most, from top to toe. About as big as the bloody lump of flesh which Pan had brought in that morning, in fact . . .

He looked over his shoulder. In the basket in the corner between the cupboard unit and the gently humming fridge, Pan sat teasing at the chunk of meat. Now and again Halford caught sight of a flash of coloured cloth amongst the blood. Could it . . .? He looked back at the shoe and put the mug on the table. Could it possibly . . .?

He drove the question away and stood up, still in his pyjamas and dressing gown. Pan looked up momentarily, then went back to tearing at the dead . . . animal. Halford gave the cat a long thoughtful look, then went upstairs to get dressed.

It had taken the warming sun a long time to raise its face above the elms and ashes beyond the bottom of the garden, and the rain-fed dew was still asparkle on the grass and in the cupped flowers.

In the pond the fish were rising, dull gold flapping gently in the water. He stood looking at them for a moment before carrying on across the lawn to the place he knew Pan liked to go, down by what had once a long time ago been a cattle shed, but which now housed the lawnmower. He wasn't even sure what it was he was looking for.

There was nothing in the lawnmower shed, or around it, except the mower and a half-full can of petrol, and a deserted starling's nest wedged in the corner of wall and roof and dangling with cobwebs. He wandered on down the garden with his hands in his duffel pockets, eyes open for anything out of the ordinary. On the way he had a look at the dying conifer, but it didn't look like recovering. It was even more brown and droopy than the last time he'd looked at it, and the bark on the thin trunk was becoming dry and peeling away from the wood beneath. He shrugged, because he could do no more than feel sorry for the tree.

Everything grew slightly wilder towards the bottom of the garden; he had two compost baskets near the fence, piled with grass clippings and leaves, and he hadn't bothered to cut the grass quite properly this far from the house. There was nothing odd here, anyway, and he went down to the fence and leaned on it and looked out across the field beyond. Everything was quiet and crisp, punctuated by birdsong. Far away, from the rookery in the woods on the other side of the field, came the tearing cry of wheeling crows. It was all so removed from the horror that his cat had brought in. A reaffirmation of the world's sanity.

Well. Whatever it was he had expected to find, it wasn't here, and he gently reproved himself for letting it worry him so. Whatever the little shoe was, it must have some kind of reasonable explanation.

He smiled slowly and looked down into the thistles and nettles on the other side of the fence, and his eye caught on a scrap of snow white, folded tiny amongst the green and brilliant purple. He put his feet on the bottom spar of the fence and leaned half his body over, reached down and caught the scrap of white between the tips of his middle and forefinger.

He straightened up and got down from the fence and held the white object up between his thumb and forefinger. It was about the size of a postage stamp, a square of white linen with a minute speck of blue in one corner. Halford felt the sane, normal, warm world start to freeze about him. What manner of being used a monogrammed handkerchief the size of a stamp?

He finally found the camera under the bed, nestling among old box files of tax forms, and eight months' back issues of the *New Musical Express*. The stand was in the wardrobe, and he still had a roll of colour film that he'd got free after processing his last set of holiday snaps. He loaded the camera in the cupboard under the stairs so light wouldn't expose the film, assembled the stand, and put the camera out on the patio where he could get a decent shot of most of the garden, setting the focus to infinity. He ran the long shutter release cable back inside and pulled the door to. It was half past twelve when he finished. He pulled up the big comfortable recliner and sat down with a big plate of luncheon meat sandwiches and a pot of coffee in front of the patio window and waited.

The day passed agonisingly slowly. Twice he developed an awful conviction that the release had failed, and he took half a dozen shots of the garden. He still wasn't certain what he expected to arrive, but he wanted to be ready when it did. The day wore on. He only got up to go to the toilet or to make more coffee. The sun sank slowly behind the house, making the shadows lengthen, the air cool. A breeze stirred the trees, rustled the dying conifer. Dusk fell slowly, became twilight; details faded, the garden receded into night. Halford felt tired and silly. His eyes hurt and his back ached from sitting too long in one position, and he still had nothing.

He got up and put a record on the hi-fi, went back and flopped into the chair again, rubbed his eyes. The slow, deep mellow opening to the Tallis Fantasia took shape in the room, swelling to occupy the silence. Halford sighed and relaxed into the cushions, reflecting quietly on how receptive to strange ideas the mind could become when left to its own devices. He picked up the last of the luncheon meat sandwiches and bit into it. Still, it had been an interesting exercise, if nothing else.

*

Light flickered on the closed curtains, dancing like firelight but pure, white. He couldn't remember falling asleep; he was just suddenly conscious of the dancing light on the curtains, and of faint bright music, chiming frosty voices singing, though he couldn't catch the words.

He lay staring at the curtains for a long time before pushing the sheets back and getting up and walking across to them. He felt oddly numb, detached, as if this was a dream, and stood for a long, long moment before pulling one of the curtains aside slightly and peeking out through the gap. After a moment he pulled it back further, then opened it completely and leaned on the sill catching his breath, fascinated in the pure crystal light.

Arranged to form a square were four tiny brilliant points of white light, nestling in the grass like incredibly bright glow worms, but wavering like windblown stars, each about six yards from the other. They were dancing inside the square, ten of them or twelve, hands joined in a ring, round and round and round, singing and dancing and skipping to some elaborate pattern. Dressed in green and grey and brown, ladies in long simple dresses, the pure light making their great butterfly wings glow iridescent blue and gold, their long hair shine like spun gold. None of them was above ten inches high.

He had put the camera in the wardrobe; it was just feet away, the means of recording the wonder, but using it never even crossed his mind. It would have been a vulgar, brutish thing to do.

The words of the song were in another language, fluid and bright, but there were woods in it, and the sharp sweep of chalk downs in the chill morning, and the measured beat of the seasons. The words were only the physical manifestation of something far greater, something awesome and terrifyingly old and beautiful, and they raged deep into his soul and took it exulting away with them to dance there on the damp grass, singing and laughing . . .

. . . he was cold, his eyes hurt. Outside everything was dark once more, the fairy ring vanished, the starlights gone, the singing silenced. In the deep old corners of his soul, the song echoed down within him, dying.

Thursday

He was up again very early the next morning, even before the eastern sky began to brighten. The dawn chorus started as he was frying some bacon and an egg and, looking out of the kitchen window, he saw the clouds begin to flush golden orange with coming dawn. Sailors' warning.

He looked around the kitchen. Pan wasn't in yet, and he wondered how he'd feel this morning if the cat brought another of them in, ripped and bloody and dead. Sad, probably. Just sad.

The bacon was taking too long to cook. He took it off the ring, turned on the grill and put the pan underneath to keep it warm. He had to know . . . He put on his Wellies and unbolted the door, unlocked it and opened it. A crisp, clean breeze gusted in past him as he stepped onto the path, and he fancied he could smell . . . them.

Out on the lawn the dew had erased any marks which might have been left there, and nothing had been left behind, no handkerchiefs or anything like that. He made a long slow search of the garden, and the sun rose above the trees across the field while he pottered about, looking under plants and turning over stones. He'd dreamed it . . . He found a stick and poked around in the compost bins, but there was nothing unusual in them. Frowning, he put his hands on his hips, doubt flowering. Across in the rookery the crows were calling, a choir with laryngitis. There didn't seem so many of them this morning. Yes, he'd dreamed a peculiarly beautiful dream, but that was all it had been.

Feeling silly, Halford turned and walked back up the garden and back to the house to have his breakfast, and behind him the crows cackled at his silliness.

When he got the typewriter out again after breakfast and sat down at it, he read through what he'd written two days before, before his mind had been taken up with other things. It seemed very silly; clumsy and naive in the extreme, and he wondered what could have possessed him to write such weak, juvenile nonsense. The words, which he had thought conveyed vivid emotional states, were cold and meaningless, just a collection of shapes arranged in parallel lines on the paper. Any emotion they suggested came from their association with it, not from description. Limited. Constricted.

A little scared now, he took out the rest of the manuscript and started to read. At first haltingly, then with a horrified fascination. Engrossed, but for the wrong reason. It was awful.

The subtle situations he had lovingly crafted for his protagonist were stiff, stilted. The dialogue, which he'd thought sharp and crafty, was ridiculous and pointless. He had thought the prose very tight, lean and sparse and cold, but it was superfluous and wandering. And the plot . . . oh God, the plot . . .

He sat back in his chair with a sigh and rubbed his eyes. Eyes still shut, he flung the sheaf of paper fluttering across the room. Some of the sheets flapped into the fire and whooshed into flame and were gone, curling scraps of ash. Others fell forlorn and creased to the carpet.

He got up slowly and put the Tallis Fantasia on the hi-fi, turned the volume up as far as it would go and went and sat down in the big recliner, pushed it back into the reclining position and lay back and shut his eyes.

The gentle, beautiful music was coarse and simple, the glorious antiphony a cheap trick. And Halford suddenly knew why. The echo of the song hadn't died. He'd heard better. He'd heard things expressed that human tongues could not match, that human minds could not possibly conceive, and all things human paled before them. And he knew it would always be like that. He could try to forget, but he'd always have the song in him, maiming all the world's beauty.

After a moment he began to cry.

zone of silence

They were scratching beyond his ceiling again. Always above the bed, always just beside the tiny ridge of raised plaster two feet out from the wall. He lay sleepless again, puffing thoughtfully on a cigarette, while the tiny claws rattled in the space between his ceiling and the floor above. A long way across the city the motorway murmured drowsily to itself, even less able to sleep than he was.

He made a face and got up in one impatient surge, and then came to a halt a few feet from the bed, uncertain what to do now he was out, the irritation fading. Above his head the tiny rattlings skittered about on the other side of the ceiling. He'd lain in bed several nights now, listening, and he was reasonably sure that there were three of the rats. Reporting the noises to the Superintendent had brought the rodent control man round, and the next day a stiff-faced Health Inspector who refused to call him by name and checked the flat matter-of-factly and then went away without comment.

The rats were still there.

The claws scrabbled again, and looking up, he could follow their progress diagonally across the ceiling to the corner above the window, then back along the wall, where they finally fell silent above his head.

Poul walked across to the window, undid the catch and slid it up. Sharp late-night air gushed into the bedroom, free for a while at least of the oppressive daytime excreta of cars and lorries. Ten storeys below the street was empty, and beyond it the park slept dark and mysterious, the slight wind-whisper of the trees just fighting its way up to him. And beyond the park and down the hill, the city, sparkling and bejewelled, lay like a precious thing on the night, cold and very beautiful. He leaned on the sill and flipped the cigarette butt out into space. It tumbled away from him, a tiny red falling star, to end in a microscopic burst of red sparks on the pavement far below.

He sighed and looked away across the city. The motorway was lost among the lights, but he could still hear its quiet thoughtful mumbling. The city too mumbled with traffic, but it was a different sound, more leisurely, drowsy. The motorway sound was of cars going to other places, leaving the bright city behind and traversing the night, but the city sound was the sound of things moving inside the brightness, like a heartbeat.

The scratching started again, directly above his head. It didn't seem persistent, as though the rats were trying to dig through, but rather as if they were just chasing round and round in the space beyond the ceiling. There was a pause in the scratching, then a slight thud, and then the scratching resumed. Poul pursed his lips and went into the living room, picked up the phone on the breakfast bar, and dialled for the Superintendent.

It rang at the other end for a long time before someone picked up the receiver and said, "Superintendent," in a drowsy, faceless, just-woken-up sort of voice.

"Hello, this is Mr Nilsson—"

"What's your room number?"

"A thousand and twenty-seven. Look, I've—"

"One. Oh. Two. Seven. I wish people would speak proper. Right. Can I help you?"

Poul shut his eyes and sighed. "Yes. I reported rats five days ago, and the rodent control operative and the Health Inspector both came and almost tore my flat up, and the rats are still there."

A moment's silence, then, "Did you fill in a QRS 226/88574?"

He had to think a long moment before realising what the Superintendent meant. "Oh, yes. Yes, you did give me a form to fill in. Look, I consider it very unhy—"

"Mmm. So you'll want a QRS 226/88574 b for this complaint, won't you?"

He took the handset away from his ear and looked at it for a moment before saying, "I want these rats got rid of," very slowly and carefully.

For the first time the voice exhibited emotion. "Well I can't do anything about it at this time of night. I'll ring the ratman tomorrow morning."

Poul said, "Wonderful," and put the phone down.

The rodent control man arrived the next morning, while he was having breakfast. He answered the door with a slice of toast and marmalade in his hand, already conscious that he'd be late when he got to the bank. The rodent control man looked prim and efficient in freshly-pressed overalls, but the effect was spoiled by the sheepish, almost schoolboy look on his face.

"Whatever you did, it didn't work," said Poul.

The rodent control man stepped into the flat. "Nobody's perfect," he said while Poul shut the door behind him.

"I had expected some improvement."

The shoulders of the blue nylon overalls shrugged. "Little buggers are developing resistances to some of our poisons."

"Can't you do anything about it?"

"You're not English, are you?" Which was a rather pointless thing to say, because Poul knew he wasn't English.

"No," said Poul.

The rodent control man nodded. "Okay. I'll get to work then."

"Good idea." Poul went back to the breakfast bar and sipped his tea.

"Could do with some Millacin," mused the rodent control man. Poul looked up. "What does that do?"

Rooting in his bag, the rodent control man looked up. "Millacin?

Oh, it suppresses the enzyme reactions in a rat's intestinal tract. Lipases and proteases, that sort of thing, you know? The ones that break down food."

Poul looked at his slice of toast and thought it through with what he liked to think of as staunch Scandinavian logic. "The rat starves to death?"

"Among other things."

Poul didn't like the way he'd said that. It implied rats dying of indigestion and constipation as well, which, he reflected, was a hell of a way to go. "It sounds a pretty nasty way to go," he said. "Even for a rat."

The rodent control man shook his head. "I'm not going to use it today, even though the little buggers don't have a resistance to it yet. It's new stuff, and I'm not authorised to use it."

"Is it very dangerous?"

The rodent control man gave a long slow smile that lifted his upper lip away from too-long incisors. "It works on people too."

Poul looked at his slice of toast and sighed. The rodent control man had quietly, efficiently put him off his breakfast.

The Superintendent met him as he made his way to the lift that evening.

"It's a QRS 226/88574 b," he said, proffering a form.

Poul looked at it, took it, read it. "Oh," he said.

"You called in the ratman, so you have to fill in this form too," he said, speaking very slowly, as if Poul was some kind of idiot.

Poul nodded a little wearily. "I'll let you have it back tomorrow," he said, making for the lift again.

"The lift is out of order. You will have to use the stairs."

Poul looked at the doors of the lift. On average, the lifts were out of order twice a day, for reasons which varied from servo failure to plain vandalism. Complaints to the Superintendent were only answered with endless complaint forms, and the lifts kept on breaking down. They seemed to typify the state of the entire block.

He'd been here six months now. After finishing a three-year business administration course at Sheffield University, he had joined the management of a large bank. Even so, he found dealing with the endless customers a rather impersonal job, not helped by the flat he had been forced to take. He had never spoken to the people living on either side of him; in fact, his ritual communication of complaint and red-tape reply with the Superintendent formed the only contact he had with anyone in the building. He knew the flat on his left was occupied by an elderly widow whose married daughter visited her every other Sunday. He didn't know who was in the flat on the other side.

He opened his eyes and something scrabbled in the dark above his head, and for a moment there in the dark, it almost seemed as if opening his eyes had started the noises off. But he knew that was silly; the rats couldn't possibly know when he was awake or when he was asleep. Still, the thought had caused a little chill of fear in his stomach. He'd heard some strange stories about rats . . .

Or were they . . .?

He'd assumed all this time that rats must be causing the noises, but it might be another small animal entirely. Mice, perhaps, or a nest of birds. It wasn't inconceivable. It could be anything. Cockroaches even. That might explain the ineffective rat poison. It might not work on insects or birds.

The scrabbling moved away across the ceiling until it was above the window, then it seemed to take on a new urgency, as if it had suddenly been focussed on a small area of ceiling. He frowned, listening intently now, and the little chill came back. It seemed to him that the tiny claws were trying to dig through . . .

. . . standing at the window, he watched the false dawn sketch in the outlines of the city. His eyes hurt, and his stomach was half full of tepid coffee. His mouth tasted as though he had been licking out ashtrays. In the bedroom the scratching noises had continued

113

unabated all night, and he couldn't bring himself to go back in. He leaned on the draining board in the kitchen and stared morosely out of the window.

The false dawn slowly blended into a gradual brightening of the sky away across the city, and there came a moment when everything seemed to tense, and then an unbearable sliver of light burst up over the rolling crest of the moors over the other side of the city, pouring light directly into the flat while the valley below and the city occupying it remained dark and mysterious.

(Everything arrested . . . everything balanced forever in a moment where the valleys lay plunged in night while dawn leapt from hill to hill, exulting, across the face of the world.)

The spell began to break. Down in the valley the glittering jewel began to go out. One by one, headlights were dipped, streetlights began to turn themselves off, and slowly, agonisingly, a great sheet of daylight began to roll down the hill towards the city as the sun lifted itself out of the east. Already it was touching the very tops of the highest buildings down below, and as he watched planes of light crept down their faces inch by inch, until the dawn had completely uncovered the city.

He rubbed his eyes, turned from the window, and looked across the room, through the open bedroom door, to the tiny section of bedroom ceiling he could just see. The scratching hadn't stopped. Whatever was making the noises, they were moving about in the daytime now.

He hadn't used the step-ladder since decorating the flat, and he had to dig around for ten minutes in the cupboard before he managed to get to it. Carrying the ladder and a big camping lantern, he opened the door and went out into the corridor. As usual, the cleaners had done their little trick of cleaning only every other floor, and had missed this one. Empty cigarette packets and paper bags were strewn across the corridor, and several doors down the abandoned newspaper wrapping of a fish and chip meal lay lodged in the joint of wall and floor like a strange newsprinted animal at bay. The corridor was cold and smelled damp and musty, and the fire doors at the end sported two broken panes of reinforced glass.

Just down the corridor from his flat there was a square trapdoor in the ceiling, where the rodent control man had gone up into the ceiling space to set his poisons. He'd walked under it every day, going to and coming from work, but now it took on a whole new significance. He set the ladder under the trapdoor and went slowly up.

The trapdoor was secured by four screws. This necessitated a twenty-minute search in the flat for a screwdriver, and when he came out again someone had stolen the ladder. By now, however, he was moving on some kind of momentum. The motion into the ceiling space had been initiated, and the momentum made him go back into the flat and come out again with one of the tall breakfast stools. It just reached, though he had to stretch.

Getting the screws out was difficult. The rodent control man had been over-zealous about replacing them, and the heads of two had been deformed. As he unscrewed them bits of dry paint flaked off the wood of the trap and fell into his eyes. He was sweating by the time he had taken all four out, and he reached up, put his hand flat against the door, and pushed.

The trapdoor lifted on all sides, unhinged, and he flipped it over to one side. Then, holding the sides of the hole and with the lantern hanging from his belt, he lifted himself with a little difficulty into the space between the ceiling and the floor above.

In the dark before he turned on the light, it was the smell he noticed first. A rich, clean smell, pungent and cold. It was horribly alien here. There should have been the cloying smell of dust, musty things, rats. This was . . . crushed grass, wind-whipped heather, cold mists lit by dawnlight, great dark forests, the sharp sweep of chalk downs in some ancient morning, wind brushing between standing stones, cold hard mountains . . .

He turned on the lantern, and the light seemed to drive the images back. He looked about him, surprised at how big the space actually was. It was high enough for him to crouch there on hands and knees. In the dimness, beams were grey parallels across the floor and ceiling, and fading a little distance away the dark thick verticals of supporting columns, the building's skeleton. Wiring channels, blocky water tanks, pipes. The place was cluttered, but one look around was enough to assure him. If there was anything living up here, he could not possibly miss seeing it. And as far as he could see, there was nothing alive here but himself.

As he moved to return to the world of light, he noticed a small pile of yellow crumbs, like breadcrumbs. The rodent control man's poison. And it hadn't been touched.

He sat for a long time in the big black leather armchair he'd bought the first day he'd been here, and thought very hard about what to do. It was his day off, so he had all day to do something positive about the scratching noises. He had an advantage over the rodent control man and the Health Inspector, because all their solutions were stock solutions. Dealing with perhaps a couple of hundred cases a week, they would develop a series of stereotyped methods, from which they could choose when they were faced with a problem. Here, though, he was fairly certain that rats were not the cause of the noises, and since he knew more about the noises and their habits than anyone else, he could plan and tailor his defence to fit, rather than choose from a set of stereotypes and hope for the best. He frowned and thought, and three cups of coffee later he had an idea.

The nearest hardware shop was twenty minutes away by bus (ten minutes spent waiting for the bus) and he was back in the flat by dinnertime with a large cardboard box in his arms. He dropped it on the kitchen table, and one of the sides burst. A couple of traps clattered out; one fell to the floor. He ignored it. Again, the motion had been initiated and its momentum kept it going. He carried the stool out into the corridor, brought the box of traps out, and lifted it up into the ceiling space, then climbed up after it.

He had around sixty traps altogether. The shopkeeper had made a tasteless joke about keeping rats as pets, which he had ignored. Crawling on hands and knees along the beams, he tried to distribute the traps evenly about the space, setting them as he went. The strange smell (a beech hanger topping a hill, the trees whispering in the breeze) seemed different now. Not stronger or weaker, but more . . . open, more free, as if an invisible hole to the outside had been enlarged and the wind (stirring the heather along a cliff-top) allowed to breathe into the space between the flats. He found it a strangely familiar (something old and free) smell, but deep inside him, something felt hunted somehow.

He finished setting the traps, climbed down and closed the trap-door, carried the stool and the empty box back into the flat, and made himself a cup of coffee. Then he relaxed, because finally the solution had been taken out of the hands of strangers. He thought perhaps he understood now why the rodent control man and the Health Inspector had upset him. They'd been fighting the battle for him, exorcising his demon for him, when it was an intensely personal thing, not a thing to be shared with strangers who didn't even think in the same language as he did.

Never mind. All that was over now. It was just him and the scratching noises. And the traps.

There was an animal squeal above his head, a desperate scrabb-ling, then another kind of scrabbling, quite different, then a thud, and faint ticking, clicking noises. He was out of bed and across the room almost before the noises registered. He grabbed the stool on the way through the door, slammed it down under the trap, jumped up, and banged the door up with his palms. Almost in the same movement, almost as part of it, he jumped up, and oh

there's a little clump of trees on the hill across the little valley, and down in the vale dark trees are crowded, a dim musty wood; the sound of their heads whispering rides up on the breeze that blows in from the great sweep of downland infinite beyond the hill and its trees. In the wood old dark things are prowling tirelessly, fearlessly, knowing that whatever happens to their world, they re-main inviolate, even if they sometimes give the impression of having gone away to some other he had to shake his head hard to drive the smell from his consciousness and concentrate on what he was doing. The effort made sweat burst out all over him, as if he had entered into some kind of physical struggle, but he finally brought his mind to bear on the matter in hand.

He lifted the camping lantern above his head, and the field of light swept about the little space, outlining the water tanks and the beams and the support pillars and the pipes, and the scattered traps. The light fell on something wet and sparkling, and he moved over to it, examined it under the yellow lamplight.

Caught dead in one of the metal traps was a large rat. Or rather, the rear third or so of a large rat. The head and most of the body had been torn off and were nowhere to be seen, leaving the tail and haunches bloody and ragged in the trap. It looked disturbingly as if it had been half-eaten, then discarded. He touched the rat with a trembling finger. It was still warm. The space was otherwise empty.

He climbed down and went back into the flat, turned on the living room lights and made for the phone. He was dialling when he heard the scrabbling start again. Much louder this time. And a soft falling sound.

Frowning, he put the phone down and went into the bedroom and turned on the light, looked instinctively up at the focus of the sound, and gasped quietly. Up on the ceiling, just where the sound was, the plaster was cracking and bulging sporadically, as if something above was pawing at it. As he watched, flakes of plaster dropped from the ceiling and fell softly to join others on the dark carpet. More fell, in larger chunks, and a tiny dark hole appeared. And he caught a faint wisp of that cold smell . . .

He opened the door with fumbling fingers, ran panting down the corridor, slippered feet brushing aside bits of paper rubbish and detritus. He reached the lift, hit the call button half a dozen times. As usual, it seemed to take far too long before the doors opened, and he threw himself inside.

The doors had already trapped him inside before his terror-muddled mind took in the little cell, and his breath froze in his chest. From floor to ceiling there were great gouges in the walls,

118

the paint and bits of metal scraped away, as if huge four-fingered claws had been raked down them. The smell still lingered here, like a breath from a spring morning. And had the Superintendent said the lift wasn't working?

No one heard him scream.

what makes
the flowers grow?

The Landrover pulled to a stop at the side of the road, and they got out. Booth spread the big map on the bonnet and examined it for a couple of moments, then looked across the bonnet and nodded at the clump of trees away across the fields. "That's it."

Ian turned and looked at the trees, then around at the crisp clear morning. "It's nice here."

Booth looked at the map again. "The wood's roughly circular, about a hundred yards from edge to edge, and it stands on a rise that averages fifteen feet above the level of the surrounding land. Trees are silver birch, beech, ash; some holly. Ground growth is mostly bracken and briar."

Ian put his hands in his duffel coat pockets and leaned back against the Landrover's bonnet and stared at the little wood. "Has anybody any idea how long it's been here?"

"It appears in photographs dated 1896 and 1930 in the local newspaper. I had the local police send me a slice off the top of a stump, and it tested out at eighty years, which was a big help."

Ian smiled and let a wisp of fog trail from his lips.

Booth consulted a small leather-bound notebook. "The man who wrote to me was very thorough, and checked everything. There's nothing living there. No burrows of any kind, or even birds' nests."

Ian looked over his shoulder at the older man. "Are you sure?"

Booth looked up from his notebook. "I trust my sources, yes."

Ian grinned and looked back at the clump of trees. The field between them and the road lay fallow; clover and grass, sparkling with melting frost. Beyond the trees, about a quarter of a mile away, was a little white farmhouse, bright in the sharp morning. Even from this distance, he knew it was empty.

"That'll be the farmhouse then," he said, nodding towards it.

Booth consulted the map again, and nodded. "Yes, that's it."

Ian stood and stared at the farmhouse, his breath clouding in front of his face. Booth folded up the map and put it back into the glove compartment before stepping round the Landrover to Ian's side. "Shall we take a look?"

Ian stepped away from the Landrover. "Yes."

The wood had a presence. It brooded, dark and cold at the edge of the field like some great creature. And old. Very, very old . . .

They stopped at the edge of the wood, and Ian put his hand against the smooth white skin of a silver birch and let his fingers explore the surface. "Screaming Copse," he said.

"That's what they call it," said Booth. "They've called it that for a very long time."

He looked round. "How long?"

Booth shrugged. "The village appears in the Domesday Book; most of the land in the area was just unenclosed common grazing land then, but there was a forest here, much, much bigger. About a mile across. Of course, it was cleared and cultivated as time went on."

"And now only the heart's left," said Ian.

Booth tapped a tree. "Just the heart."

Ian was silent for a long while before saying, "Let's have a look at the farmhouse."

Booth looked across at him. "Are you sure?"

He scratched his head. "Yes. We can come back and check the wood later."

Booth nodded. "All right."

The farmhouse was a quarter of an hour's unhurried walk across the waking fields. Ian noted that most of the fields were fallow, as if the entire farm, land and all, had been abandoned.

The cobbled farmyard was empty, clear of animals and manure. The outbuildings were empty too, and a big modern-looking milking parlour had been stripped of all its equipment. Ian sniffed and wrinkled his nose. It didn't even smell like a farm any more.

Booth stood a few feet away, looking about him, caught in a wash of sunrise over the buildings. "A farm shouldn't get like this," he said almost to himself.

Hands in pockets, Ian walked up beside him and stood in the light. The farmyard was a cobbled landscape of light and shade, complex but empty. Planes of light and dark and smeared shadows. But empty.

"I know what you mean," he said.

"Getting anything?"

Ian tapped his lips with a forefinger, then shook his head. "It's never much more than a feeling anyway. Nothing you could depend on."

"But you felt something out at the wood."

He frowned thoughtfully, shook his head again. "Nothing I can identify." He took a packet of cigarettes from the back pocket of his jeans, took one out. "Got a light?"

Booth handed him his matches. "If anything bad had happened, you'd feel it though?"

"Sometimes. If it was bad enough." He lit up, took a long peaceful drag. "You should have brought Alan. He's much better at this psychometry lark."

Booth nodded. "And he has a wife who objects to being dragged to every haunted house in the country."

Ian blew out smoke. "I don't know why you wanted me here anyway. I'm not picking up anything you can't."

"You forget I'm doing a paper on environmental psychometry as well as looking into this little phenomenon."

Ian grunted. "Yes, I forgot."

Booth looked at his watch. "The caravan should be here by now."

Ian walked over to the farmhouse, tried the door. It was unlocked;

the windows were dirty and uncurtained. The bottom of the door, warped with the damp, scraped on the step as he pushed it open, and he sniffed cold damp air, and knew at once the house was empty. No, not just empty . . . Abandoned. In a state of great terror.

He stepped back from the doorway, but he could feel the cold heavy air gushing out, almost tangible, like fear. He blinked. "Yes," he said. "Something bad did happen here." And that despite the fact that the tobacco would suppress the reaction. He took another drag. "It might take a while for everything to sort itself out. All I get at the moment is . . . loud noise . . . screaming. Panic." When he'd been younger, he'd thought that emotions stuck somehow to buildings and furniture like a smell, and that his nose was the only one sensitive enough to smell them. Five years performing for various university and private research groups had forced half a dozen theories on him, some plausible, many silly. But sometimes he still went back to his old theory. This farmhouse *smelled* of terror; so much so that he felt a tiny rush of adrenalin within him, almost in sympathy.

Booth took out his pipe, filled it carefully and lit it, puffed reflectively and paced slowly across the cobbles. "Two years ago this was a thriving little holding. Some good arable land, a profitable dairy herd. A nice little business. It was owned by George Miller and his wife, with a seasonally variable number of farmhands."

Ian looked about him. Two years, and the emotions had still been powerful enough to affect him. Something very bad had happened. "Mm," he said.

Booth shrugged. "And one night twenty months ago something happened here. George Miller and four workmen were found dead the next morning, and his wife was found out there in the fields, stark staring mad. She hasn't said a word since; they have to feed her through a tube."

Ian shook his head and shut his eyes, but there was only confusion here; blind terrified confusion. Screaming blind panic.

"They weren't sure it was her at first," Booth was saying. "Alison Miller had a fine head of red hair, you see, and the woman they found in the fields had hair that was white. Snow white."

Ian scowled. "I wonder why they call it Screaming Copse."

The caravan was parked behind the Landrover when they got back. Richard was chocking the wheels and all the doors were open. It was a big long caravan, an old converted mobile library caravan that Booth had rescued from a wrecker's in Northampton. Richard's wife Jo was inside making coffee.

"Having fun?" Booth asked as they climbed the stile.

Richard straightened up. "Anything?"

They crossed the road, and Ian went up the steps into the caravan. Booth leaned on the side of the caravan and looked back at the wood and the farmhouse. "I think I almost know how Ian feels. It's very, very strange."

"You think we'll find anything?"

Booth shrugged and knocked his pipe out on the wheel arch. "We'll have to see."

"What does Ian think?"

"Ian isn't sure. I think he needs time to get the feel of the place, that's all."

Richard pursed his lips. "Do we really need him?"

Booth shrugged. "Do we really need you? Or me, for that matter? He's done investigations with me before, so he's just as qualified to be here as you are. Being able to read a location is in many ways just a bonus."

"Thanks a lot," said Ian, coming back down the steps with a steaming mug of coffee.

"No offence meant, of course," Booth said with a smile.

Ian sat down on the bottom step. "Of course."

After coffee they unpacked the equipment and checked that nothing had been broken in transit, then Ian and Richard did a thorough check of the wood while Booth and Jo went into the village to check the local newspaper. In the evening they held a council of war.

Booth sat back in his chair and said, "Well, gentlemen?"

Ian and Richard looked at each other. "You tell him," said Ian, cradling his mug in his hands.

Richard sniffed. "I'd been assuming—hoping, rather—that all or most of the local data you'd collected was wrong somehow. Exaggerated. After all, the only background you had was someone you'd never seen sending you clippings from the paper and what he'd found out."

Booth smiled slowly. "Yes."

Richard looked at the tablecloth. "The hill's just about circular, with a rounded top. And there's nothing alive in that wood."

"Except the trees," Ian put in.

Jo sat back. "How about that," she said to Booth.

"You were right about that," Richard went on. "No burrows, no birds. Not even an old nest."

"Not even any insects," said Ian.

Booth nodded. "What about tree parasites?"

Ian shook his head. "Not a one. No fungi, lichen or creepers. The trees are much too healthy. Like I said, there's nothing but trees living in that wood."

"If you count bracken and briar as trees," said Richard.

Booth sipped at his coffee. "What about the arrangement of the trees?"

Richard shrugged. "Looks random to me."

Ian nodded. "Yes."

Booth took a long thoughtful breath, exhaled. "We've found out why they call it Screaming Copse."

On 18th June, 1796, a carpenter named Peter Smith was making his way back to his village on horseback after attending his brother's wedding fifteen miles away in another village. It had been a fine day, but the sun was setting now and he was anxious to get home. Understandable considering the number of vagrants wandering the country. It was a fine sunset, all red and gold, but now that things were cooling and the sun had hidden itself behind the horizon he was wanting to reach the village.

The rough road took him by a stretch of woodland known locally as Coope's Copse, and being a local, if he noticed it at all, it was just in passing. Then his horse came to a stop.

Perhaps he frowned, pursed his lips, tried to nudge the animal on, favoured it with a few well-chosen phrases. The horse stood where it was. Motionless.

Peter Smith was still just a little drunk after the wedding party, otherwise he might have had more sense than to get down off his horse and leave it there. It still didn't move. The village was only half an hour away, and he set off through the wood towards home.

He was found the next morning face down on the wood's edge, his clothes torn and his face bloody. Everybody thought he had been set upon by ruffians and beaten senseless, for he seemed bemused and terrified and was unable to answer questions. A great patch of blood at the side of the road marked where his horse might have stood, but the animal was never found. It was a month before the vicar realised that Peter Smith wasn't mad. He was stone deaf.

Later, he wrote down most of his story, but refused to say what had happened after he had left his horse. However, years later, on his deathbed, Peter Smith indicated that pen and paper were to be given to him, and he wrote five words:

the wood screamed at me

Booth sat back and lit his pipe. Jo got up and plugged the kettle in for more coffee. Ian looked into his empty mug. "The wood screamed at me," he murmured. On that June evening all those years ago, in the fading afterglow of a lovely sunset . . .

"And the name stuck," said Richard.

"Screaming Copse," said Ian.

"And it hasn't said a word since," Jo said from the side.

"Trees can't scream," said Richard.

Ian looked out of the window and across the fields to the wood. "If they did, that's where they'd be," he said quietly.

"We were very fortunate," said Booth. "The story appeared in a 1930 copy of the local newspaper. 'Folk Tales of Our Area'. Josephine found it."

Jo smiled and gave a little bow. "Genius supplied free," she said.

Richard looked at Booth. "You think that's what happened to the farm, don't you?"

Booth draped one arm over the back of his chair. "Something similar."

"It's over a quarter of a mile away," said Richard.

"It's the nearest human habitation," said Booth.

Ian turned from the window. "It's also comfortably within the old boundary of the forest, before all the trees were cleared."

Richard looked from one to the other. "You're letting your imagination run away."

Booth took his pipe out of his mouth and looked at the tiny hearth of the bowl. "They never found George Miller's dairy herd either."

Richard lowered the camera. "I think it's a tumulus."

Booth nodded. "Yes, that would make some sense. A nice uncomplicated Bronze Age ghost manifestation."

"What's the historical evidence to back it up?" said Ian.

Booth pouted. "Very little, I'm afraid. The village church is Norman, and some Roman coins were found a couple of miles from here, but that's about it."

"However," said Jo, sitting on the bottom step, "there's evidence in old church records in villages around here that before Christianity got here the local vegetation rites were centred somewhere in this area. Spring festivals, rites to the Corn God, that sort of thing."

Ian looked at the camera in Richard's hands, then across at the Copse. "Do you really think there's something in there that ate George Miller's cows?"

Booth smiled. "Now you're adding things of your own. I only said they never found the herd." He scratched the back of his head. "I'm just thinking what a smashing place the centre of a wood would be for the burial of the Corn God's priest."

"Planted in there to be reborn with the wood every spring," Jo mused.

"That's just speculation," said Ian.

Booth shrugged. "I don't know. The Corn God's rites are associated with a great amount of energy, so the priest would command a good deal of kudos. His funeral must have been something to see. Who knows what the other priests might have done to make sure his grave wasn't disturbed?"

Richard sighed, shook his head. "This is silly."

"We can soon find out," said Booth.

Richard nodded. "Magnetometer," he said, going up the steps.

Ian looked at Booth. "Anything else you've forgotten to tell us?"

Booth tapped his pipe out on his palm. "There was a very bad thunderstorm here the night George Miller and his farmhands died," he said speculatively.

"So the Copse could have screamed again, and nobody would have heard."

Booth shrugged. "That would depend on how loud it screamed, wouldn't it?"

"What are we going to do if this hypothetical priest's spirit takes a passing fancy to us?"

Booth shook his head. "I don't know."

Ian looked across at the wood. "Nice," he said.

They spent the rest of the afternoon and most of the evening beginning a magnetic survey of the hill. If it was a tumulus, then anything buried inside the hill would cause a variation in the local magnetic field. A burial chamber would cause another kind of variation. By now Booth was becoming very hot on the idea of the hill being some kind of burial mound, if not of a priest, then of some ancient chieftain. He and Richard and Ian moved the magnetometer about inside the wood, while Jo sat under a hedge with a big sheet of paper pinned to a board, compiling a magnetic map of the hill, occasionally looking out from under the brim of her big floppy hat. Things went well, and by the time the light began to fail they had a reasonable map. When they packed up for the night Booth took the map from Jo, frowned at it, then took it back to the caravan and wouldn't let anyone see it.

'He's hiding something," Richard said as they lugged the heavy magnetometer back across the field.

Ian wrinkled his nose. "Puts a little spice into his life, I expect."

"What do you think it is?"

"He's probably found out that it isn't a tumulus after all."

"It isn't a tumulus after all," said Booth.

"Told you so," Ian murmured to Richard.

"Pardon?" said Booth.

Ian shook his head. "Just thinking out loud." He put his forearms on the table and leaned over the map spread out on the tabletop, held down at the edges by marmalade jars and toast racks. He frowned. "It looks like a stone circle," he said. "But that's silly."

"I don't think so," said Booth.

Ian chewed his bottom lip. "But all these signals are the same shape. Rectangular, like the top of a standing stone. They're all upright."

"Which brings me inescapably to one conclusion," said Booth.

"They were deliberately buried in the hill," said Jo, crunching her toast.

Booth sighed gently and brushed crumbs off the map. "Nine stones arranged in a perfect circle inside the hill. No burial chambers, no bodies, no pottery. Just the stones."

"Well," said Ian. "That blows your Corn God theory, doesn't it?"

Booth smiled. "Well, it gives it a knock, anyway."

Ian said, "How deep down are they?"

Booth pursed his lips. "Not more than six feet, down to the top of the stones, anyway. I can't tell how tall they might be."

Ian sat back and looked out of the window at the fresh, crisp morning. "Well they sure as hell aren't a Stone Age observatory," he said. "Who the hell would bury a stone circle?"

Booth shrugged. "And remember that the Copse is only the heart of what was a much bigger forest."

"Maybe it's some lost Stone Age tribe who enjoyed digging holes in the middle of woods," said Jo.

Booth pursed his lips, as though he was considering it as a valid possibility, then shook his head. "No, I shouldn't think so."

"So it's not the hill then," said Richard.

"I couldn't tell you, to tell the truth," said Booth. "I can't see a stone circle buried in the ground being responsible for all these phenomena, to be honest."

"If you see what he means," said Ian.

Richard shook his head. "Not really."

Ian got up from the table. "I'm going to have a look at the farm again."

Booth nodded. "I'll come with you."

"No, don't bother. I'm a big boy now."

Booth smiled, then started to laugh.

He had to pass the wood on the way to the farm, and he stood for five minutes just looking. Again, the wood had *presence*; he could feel it there if he shut his eyes. Whatever had happened, the wood had something to do with it, somehow . . . But the farm was a quarter of a mile away. Had the trees uprooted themselves and walked there and back? Not very likely, he decided. But if they were dealing with some kind of energy that drove people mad or deaf and made horses and cows vanish, where was it coming from? The trees might be channelling it, but it had to be coming from somewhere. Booth maintained that all psychic phenomena were manifestations of various energy states, and he could argue the point until his opponents faltered. But standing here it seemed very unlikely. Unless the wood plugged itself into the lightning, of course . . .

He leaned back against the hedge and looked sidelong at the wood. Unless the wood plugged itself into the lightning . . .

"I thought you'd gone to the farm," said Booth.

Ian bent over the table and the map spread out on it. "I've had an idea."

Booth put the kettle down, came over to the table. "Go on."

Ian put out his index finger and tapped the battered concentric system of fine lines which made the map look like a big, complex target, with its centre dead in the middle of the buried stone ring.

"It's been staring us in the face. If we hadn't been looking for bodies and things we'd have seen it straight away."

"What are you talking about?" Richard said in a tired voice.

Ian tapped the map again. "A magnetic anomaly centred on the circle."

"So?" said Jo.

"So suppose it's caused by an electrostatic field running through the ground between the stones. Like an electromagnet. Powered by electric storms."

"Ah," Booth nodded. "I see now. But they'd have to be super-conductors for that to work. Even if they were metal, they'd have to be somewhere down around the temperature of liquid nitrogen." He looked at Ian and lifted an eyebrow.

"Okay. Assume some kind of capacitance, just to keep the effect idling over. And when there's a lot of electrical activity, it triggers it."

Richard grunted. "Well, that's the daftest thing I've ever heard anyway."

"Well, that's where your manifestation of energy is coming from," Ian said to Booth. "That's what I reckon, anyway."

"Like a big battery," Jo mused.

Booth frowned at the map. "And when this electromagnetic eddy begins to intensify?"

"Why not?" said Ian. "A huge electromagnetic disturbance could affect the brain. That might account for your deaths and deaf-ness and insanity."

Booth nodded and murmured, "Yes," very quietly.

"But not the cows and Peter Smith's horse," said Richard. "You don't seriously believe this nonsense, do you?"

Booth looked up and chewed his bottom lip. He nodded. "Yes," he said thoughtfully.

Richard heaved a great sigh and sat back in his chair. "You're both nuts."

Ian looked at him. "I can prove it too."

"How?"

"Turn it on ourselves. Take the generator and run a current into the circle. As much as we can manage."

Richard shook his head. "You're out of your mind."

"I'm fascinated," said Booth. "Yes, I like it, Ian. It's a smashing idea. It might be wrong, but I'm willing to try."

Richard took his cigarettes out of his pocket and put them on the table. "Suppose you're right, just for the sake of argument. Assuming the circle's the cause of all this trouble, should we turn this thing on again?"

"You want to see me proved wrong, don't you?" Ian said.

Richard gave him a long thoughtful look, then shrugged. "It's up to you if you want to turn this project into a fantasy. Just don't blame me if it goes wrong."

Ian smiled. "It's a deal."

It took Ian most of the morning to dig down to the top of one of the stones. Richard refused to help on the grounds that it was Ian's idea after all, and his responsibility alone. The extent of his morning's exertions was to wheel the portable generator across the field to where Ian was digging.

"Reached Australia yet?" he asked cheerfully.

Ian, neck deep in his hole, looked up wrathfully. "If you won't help, don't knock it."

Richard grinned. "Are you ready yet then?"

Ian looked at his feet, where he had uncovered the top of the stone. About five feet down. "Yes. Plug the cable in, will you?"

Richard nodded, plugged the long cable into the generator and handed the coil down to Ian. The end of the cable had been bared, the copper bright against the rough stone. He spread the three copper cores across the stone and piled earth on top. Then he climbed out of the hole, grabbed the spade and began filling in.

"I still think you've flipped your top," said Richard.

Still shovelling, Ian gave a little shrug. "It's just an idea."

Richard looked across the field to where Booth was setting up the grey cabinets of the detectors. Beside him Jo was setting up the cameras, two video and four automatic stills, controlled from a single control unit and all aimed at the wood. In the wood itself, positioned above the centre of the buried ring, was the magnetometer and half a dozen other instruments, connected to the detectors by a multiple line of thick cable. "Well you've certainly sold him," said Richard.

Ian finished piling earth into the hole, stuck the spade into the ground, and stretched gratefully. "He's probably realised what a genius I am."

Richard pursed his lips. "If he has, I question his judgement."

Ian looked at him and flashed a perfectly charming smile. "Go over and tell them I'm ready, will you?"

Richard nodded and walked away across the field to the others, and after a moment Ian saw Booth raise his hand. He turned to the generator, checked all the connections for the last time, switched on fuel feed and turned the flywheel once to prime the motor. Then he put one foot on the generator's tubular frame, took hold of the starter toggle and pulled hard.

The generator turned over, coughed and stopped. He frowned, checked everything again, then pulled the starter once more. This time the motor turned over a couple of times and idled to a stop. He let the springs wind the cable back onto the drum, and looked up for a moment at the trees, and it struck him how odd it was to be using machines to investigate something as old and obviously natural as this wood, to be almost forcing a confrontation between the things he understood and the things he didn't . . .

He took hold of the toggle again and pulled, and the motor caught, a shuddering animal roaring that climbed away and filled the cold bright air. He adjusted the throttle valve, made sure there was plenty of fuel, then put his hands in his pockets and without looking back walked over to the others.

Booth puffed on his pipe. "Do stop pacing about," he said.

Ian pushed his hands hard into the linings of his pockets and forced himself to sit in one of the camping chairs. "Damn," he murmured under his breath.

Richard took a deep breath of cold, clear October evening air. All the recording instruments were silent, the faintly luminous oscilloscope screens still. He sat back and twiddled his thumbs. "Hmm."

Ian shot him a poisonous glance and started to say something bad. Booth lifted his hand, and the bad thing died in Ian's throat. Booth continued the movement and adjusted a knob on the scope in front of him, then sat back, and the tension had been exorcised.

Across the darkened fields the Copse was a chaos-topped shadow, marginally darker than the infinity of deep cold sky. Seemingly dancing in the air above it were hard, frosty bright stars. The alien animal cry of the generator echoed away into the night.

Ian looked at his watch and made a little grunting sound, crossed his arms. "Damn and blast."

"What time is it?" said Booth.

"Half-seven."

Booth shrugged and stood up. "Oh well," he said, "it was worth a try, Ian." And he went away across the field to turn the generator off.

It had rained the next morning when Ian crawled out of his tent and went into the caravan. The others had finished breakfast, and there was a polite silence as Ian came in. Jo put some more bread in the toaster for him, then went outside with Richard to dismantle the equipment.

Booth filled his pipe slowly and lovingly while Ian lit his first cigarette of the day and proceeded to do a reasonable impersonation of a man coughing his lungs up.

"You smoke too much," said Booth, lighting his pipe.

"You hypocrite," Ian said without any feeling.

Booth looked at his pipe and nodded. "Sad but true," he assented.

Ian sat looking at the creaking, popping toaster. "Go on," he said. "Tell me I was wrong."

Booth puffed on his pipe. "You're intelligent enough not to need telling."

He pursed his lips. "Bloody silly idea to start with," he said.

"Oh, of course it wasn't, Ian; come on. It was a completely original, inventive idea. It just didn't work, that's all. History is full of ideas that didn't work."

Ian sighed. "I feel so bloody silly, though."

Booth shrugged. "It's academic now, anyway."

Ian looked at him. "Mm?"

"Oh, I got a letter this morning from the Millers' son. He's away in York at university. He's withdrawing his permission for us to investigate the incident. Says we're dredging up too much emotional memory." He puffed on his pipe again. "I can't really say I blame him."

Ian looked at the toaster, then at the table. "Oh, for pity's sake," he said quietly.

"Well, I suppose he does have to go and see his mother in the hospital."

Ian got up from the table and took the toast out of the toaster, put one slice on a plate and crunched the other dry. "So we're off again."

"It looks that way."

"Without learning anything."

Booth shrugged. "Oh, I don't know. We do know about the stones in the hill."

"And without permission we can't do a blind thing."

"Not really."

"When are we going?"

"There's no hurry. I thought about eleven. We can have dinner in the pub in the village and then carry on back to London."

Ian sighed. Back to London; back to endless universities, an eternal round of tests for scientists whose numbers were so great that they eventually became faceless and who treated him in roughly the same manner. When Fort said "I think we're property", he could have been talking about the thousand or so 'talents' under investigation.

Ian put down his toast. "I'm going for a walk."

For all that Booth had said, the wood didn't feel quite the same today. In the crisp fresh damp of the morning the trees whispered softly in the light breeze, as if in quiet mockery.

He walked slowly through the little wood, shutting his eyes occasionally and trying to reach out. Something certainly felt different, though it could have been his imagination, so subtle did the change feel. He sat down in the middle of the wood and looked between the trees and watched the others packing up, far away across the field. It all seemed to have been so desperately futile.

Something bright in the twig-litter on the ground beside him caught his eye, and he stirred a finger amongst the twigs to retrieve it. He caught it between thumb and forefinger, and lifted it up to eye level, a two-inch length of bright, bare copper wire from one of the cable cores. Almost unconsciously, he put it in his pocket instead of throwing it away. It didn't belong here. The machines didn't belong here. He didn't belong here.

He got up and put his hands in his pockets, and walked away across the fields to where the caravan and Landrover waited to carry him back to London.

A clock was striking two o'clock far away in the cool air, like some kind of ghost bell, and the young woman pushing the pram stopped a moment to adjust her watch. Ten minutes away, her mother would be preparing lunch, a little late because they had been into town earlier.

The young woman took the moment and extended it, pausing to look across the empty fields, and being a local, if she noticed Screaming Copse at all, it was just in passing. What she did notice was a tiny bright splash of blue in the hedgerow, and when she stooped, with difficulty because of her obvious pregnancy, she saw that the splash of colour was a little bunch of bluebells, some of them just-opened buds. It surprised her a little, in this fag-end of October, though she had seen snowdrops the day before in her garden. She stood up and looked at the wood. The rich golden Autumn foliage was gone, replaced by glossy, dark green. She felt a slow surge of wonder begin within her. Summer leaves on an Autumn wood.

She stooped again and touched one of the bluebell buds gently, without suspecting the untold megatons of energy that Nature stored in bud and seed, without knowing that the key to all those megatons was close by, without suspecting the agony of Summer being forced on Autumn.

Inside her, the child stirred, and she straightened up again and held the pram's handle until it was still. It was three months before the baby was due.

She took the handle with both hands again and resumed her slow walk to her mother's house, and behind her in the fields clover began to bloom and charge the air with its heady scent; buttercups became bright tiny explosions, the hedges whispered quietly their agony, and the Copse began to beat and thrash with a wind which wasn't there.

That evening, the Copse screamed, and everything living for fifteen miles heard its voice. Finally, the Corn God had a new flock.

encroachments

When he woke again, it was different; something had changed. He lay in bed with his eyes open, staring at the ceiling and listening to the low branch scrape the wall of the house. Something subtly different, but he could not make out what. Outside the wind howled and roared, primal and keen in the dark night. The wood beside the house beat and thrashed with it like an ocean against high cliffs. If he closed his eyes the house could be drifting out at sea, lost without trace in the night.

He frowned up in the darkness at the featureless ceiling, trying to work out what had woken him, but he still couldn't make out what had changed, and now he had been called up out of sleep it was impossible to go back. He turned over on his side and picked the alarm clock up off the floor. The luminous hands indicated five-thirty. He scowled at them, put the clock back on the floor and rolled out of bed.

He didn't bother putting any lights on downstairs now that his eyes were night-adapted. It seemed wrong to wake the house as well.

The kitchen was transfigured. Cold silver moonlight shone through the window and onto the carpet in a great bar, igniting the shiny sink unit, splashing the corner of a cupboard, a whole new fairy landscape of dark and cold light.

He plugged in the kettle, filled up the night before, and left it to boil. He swilled out the teapot and added fresh tea, took a clean mug from the cupboard and spooned in sugar, then left everything on the side and stood at the sink and stared out into the garden. The moonlight worked here too, making it look strange to him, touched here and there by pure light. Cold and alien as the face of the moon which lit it.

Away down the garden and across the fields the trees whipped and thrashed in torment with the wind, and it plucked and beat at the house, impotently trying to drive it across the face of the world. It seemed totally unreasonable that it shouldn't blow the bright cold moon away across the sky and beyond the horizon.

The kettle drummed and spluttered noisily. He went across and unplugged it, poured the water into the pot, put the top on and popped the cosy over the pot and left it to mash. A couple of minutes later, he lifted the cosy and poured himself a mug of hot, strong, sweet tea. He sat in the silent kitchen listening to the wind cry and the branch scrape the wall, and slowly drank his tea. Completely at peace.

Exactly half an hour before dawn (he checked the time) the wind died to a gentle whisper and fell silent. Dawn was about half-six around this time of year, and he was on his third mug of tea when the sun burst, molten gold, over the grey slag hills of the open-cast mine four miles away and flooded everything with warm light. He sat in the kitchen and watched the new dawn blush in the sky, then went upstairs to get dressed.

The post arrived at half past seven, which was the earliest he'd ever had his post delivered. He supposed his was the first stop on the morning's rounds, but he'd never asked. He hadn't been here long enough to, really. He'd only ever seen his postman once, anyway. He was back in the kitchen, finishing a plate of bacon and egg and sausage and turned when he heard the letters whisper on the hall mat: two short white envelopes, a long white one and a long buff one. He sat half-turned on the chair, one arm over the back, and guessed. The buff envelope was quite large, maybe a royalty statement, though he couldn't remember if he was due one or not. The two white ones could be from anybody really, though he was about due one from Julie, wherever she was at the moment. The long white one was probably from his publisher.

He grinned. Now then.

He went and took the letters from the mat, brought them back to the table and opened the buff one with a butter knife and extracted the slip of paper with his fingertips. He frowned. A bill from the typewriter shop in town, which had had his new electric typewriter delivered the day before. He put the bill on the table and weighted it down with the butter dish.

One of the small white envelopes had a Cologne postmark and was from his father. Dear Colin, having a wonderful time wish you were here, Johannes. He sighed and scratched his head. His father was spending more and more time over there nowadays, ostensibly on holiday, but he rather suspected that the old man wanted to move back to Cologne and finish his life in the city where he had been born. He slipped the letter under the bill. One day, Papa. When I have enough money. Next year maybe.

The other small white envelope was from Julie, just a short note to let him know where she was and that she was all right. She was in Braemar. She didn't say why.

The third envelope was from his publisher, promising him a look at the cover proofs of his new book. Again.

Well, that was the first thrill of the day gone. He frowned and looked at the window. That damn branch was scraping the wall again. He sat for a whole minute staring at his plate before finally getting fed up with the thing.

The garden was triangular, which was a ridiculous shape for a garden, but it was one of the things which had attracted him to the house in the first place. The garden was quite large, the house itself forming the base of the triangle, and the other two sides were formed by hedges, separating the garden from the fields beyond. From his bedroom window the garden seemed like the prow of a great ship, breasting a wild untidy sea.

On the left of the house, growing almost up to it, was a dense little wood of old oaks and elms, dark and mysterious. He'd walked in it the first day he had been here, and found it to be just a little clump of old, almost dead trees, and from that day on its mystery was gone.

One tree actually grew up to the wall of the house; an ancient twisted oak which had over the years reached out a branch to touch the stone of the wall, and every time the wind blew this branch scraped and shivered on the wall, as if the tree was trying to scratch its way through and into the house. It had only just begun to bother him.

Armed with a big logging saw, he carried the step-ladder across the garden to the stile in the hedge, then round the side to the oak, and set the ladder up beneath the branch. Taking off his jacket, he put it on the ground beside the steps, took up the saw, and climbed until the branch was at about chest height. He lifted the big saw, rested the blade on the branch, and began to saw. In the wood, the trees began to murmur softly in the breeze . . .

He was sweating when he finished. The oak was tougher than he had thought, but the branch finally crashed dryly to the ground, rustling and clawing at the side of the house as it fell. The tree looked oddly lopsided without it, like a man with only one arm, but at least it wouldn't disturb him any more. Climbing back down the ladder, he noticed older scars on the tree, where other branches had been cut away, and he wondered why the branch hadn't been taken care of then. Never mind; he'd done it now. He dragged the heavy branch by degrees a few yards away from the tree, then decided it was too old and heavy to do anything with, so he left it where it was. He packed the step-ladder up and carried it back to the outplace, and stood for a moment looking away across the fields at the ashen grey blight of the great open casting. The deep dull roar of the machines reached him dimly on the breeze. The plan, he had heard, was to landscape the area after all the coal had been extracted, and to make the workings into a park or recreation complex of some kind. When it was finished, ten or fifteen years from now, this area would benefit from a boom in trade. Meanwhile, it was a malignant sore on the country's face. And looking at it across this bright warm day, an idea slowly triggered off inside him.

He wasn't sure of the size of the workings; several thousand acres, certainly. A lot of this had once been pasture, if rather poor pasture, but now it was a grey sterile waste, the earth ripped open and the gaping wound allowed to fester. It spread down into the wide, shallow valley, stopping at the edge of the town, and up across the curve of the hill. In the valley the landscape was dominated by two great stepped hills, their flat heads tilted a little, around which great lorries made their tireless way all day long, taking spoil to the top and returning empty.

From the road which ran down the hill to the town, the workings looked huge and empty, and from this distance there was no life to be seen, no movement except for the graders and lorries, and the jib of a huge dragline just moving into view from behind one of the hills. No human life could be seen. It might have been an alien world, dominated by machines.

He took pictures. Julie's Pentax still had about three-quarters of a seventy-two shot roll of film in it, and by the time he got back home he had used them all recording the extent of the working and every aspect of its form. An old canal embankment ran along one edge of the open casting, where it splashed up the side of the hill, so he was able to get right up to the workings, and using the tele-photo lens he was able to get shots of all the machines in use on the site. And yet, he had only a handful of photographs of human beings. It was a machine-dominated environment, and in a way that seemed fitting. It wasn't a place for people.

Close to, he realised that the greyness of the open cast was not actually ash, as it seemed from a distance, but clay, in great thick heavy clods, random minerals making streaks of yellow and red and darker grey. The clay was ripped and tumbled, glistening like a thick sea. He took a final couple of photos of lorries taking the coal out of the main gate, then went home.

Went down to the open cast today, spent all afternoon photographing it. It's a strange, frightful environment, like a Nash painting of the Western Front but without even the dead trees to give the memory of life. It's as if nothing ever lived there. Just the machines going back and forth blindly, unquestioning, ripping deeper and deeper. It struck me as disquieting that such devastation can be so close beneath the surface. All you have to do is peel back the green, the life. And it's such a thin covering . . .

He sat back and chewed the rubber on the end of his pencil while he read through the diary entry, written to go with the photographs. It seemed to sum up his feelings about the workings, but it didn't say everything. It didn't annotate the thin, lonely sound of the wind crying between the spoil hills, or the emotionless drumming of the machines, or . . .

He frowned at his notebook, and out of his unconscious mind a bright idea came flying. And something was wrong as well . . .

He looked up, and tried to sort out the sense impressions. It took him a couple of moments to realise that the wind had risen, and the branch was scratching on the wall again. Which was totally unreasonable because he had cut the branch down that morning.

The wind was quite strong now. The little wood thrashed with it, and it tousled his hair with insubstantial fingers, flapped his jacket about him as he walked across the garden and crossed the stile.

The tree was just about as he had left it; it bore the pale circular scar where he had amputated the branch. But there was still a branch touching the wall of the house. He stood, hands in pockets, looking at the twisted old tree, trying to remember. He was certain that when he'd finished that morning there had been nothing touching the house; no part of the tree at all. And he must be wrong. His memory must be faulty in some way. He must have missed a branch.

He walked slowly around the tree, looking up at it. It occurred to him that apart from the branch now touching the house, there was something else wrong with the tree. The stub of branch he had cut that morning seemed to be pointing the wrong way now; it seemed to be turned a little away from the house, pointing more towards the garden. The soil around the base of the tree seemed disturbed too, and there were some roots exposed which he couldn't remember seeing before. It looked as if . . . as if the tree had turned itself to bring the other branch into contact with the house. But that was silly. He turned and went to get the saw and the steps.

He set the steps up again, climbed them to the top, put one hand on the branch, and with the other rested the saw on it as he had done that morning. As he did so, the wind seemed to make the whole tree shiver, and he had to pause a moment to catch his balance before starting to cut. The same gust of wind which had blown the tree made the wood beyond whisper and moan. He narrowed his eyes and bent to the saw. This time, he was determined to make sure.

Later, when he'd finished and dragged the cut branch a fair distance from the tree and made absolutely certain that no others could touch the house, he put a fresh sheet of paper into the new electric typewriter, made himself comfortable with a couple of tins of beer within easy reach, and put his fingers to the keys . . .

A long time ago this country was almost covered with forests. Huge forests; dark old forests, forests that would make your heart cry just to look on them. Forests to thick in places that the easiest, and sometimes only, way to travel the country was on the unwooded high ground. Berkshire's Ridge Way is a case in point, the old chalk path that runs all along the crest of the Chilterns. So, men didn't travel the forests much, and they looked down from their paths into the old dark, whispering woods and created a whole pantheon of creatures to inhabit them. Elves, dwarves, trolls, wood spirits, earth spirits, sprites, Jacks-in-the-green. And perhaps also older, darker things which they wouldn't, or couldn't put a name to. Perhaps all these stories were grounded in some fact, perhaps not. It would be nice to think they were, but the chances are they're just fantasy . . .

He sat back and rubbed his eyes. Outside the wind thrashed and shouted indignantly in the wood as dusk fell. It had taken him an hour and a half to finish this little section, but he was after all just getting his thoughts in order for something else. He wasn't sure quite what, but all the elements were there.

He was out of beer; the ringpulls rattled emptily in both cans. He sat and pondered for a moment, then he turned off the typewriter and picked up the cans and went to make dinner. He'd done enough for one day.

In the thrash and cry of the windy night, the thunder of the great mining machines came dully into his sleep. Slowly, painfully opening his eyes, he turned over and groped on the carpet for the clock. His fingers stumbled on it, tumbled it over on its back, and he hung half out of bed looking at the hands. One in the morning, and they were still mining out there in the beat of the wind. God, didn't they ever stop?

He got out of bed and went to the window and pulled the heavy curtain back. Outside, the night sky was mottled silver and grey, the moon drifting in and out of fragmented cloud, the triangular garden seeming again like the dark prow of a ship breasting a pale ghostly sea.

Away on his right were the tiny bright lights of the workings, scattered at random on the spoil hills. He had imagined them to be for winter, when the nights drew in and darkness fell before knocking off time, but they didn't seem to want to knock off. Moving between the tiny blue-white arclights were the duller yellow headlights of the big lorries and graders, and microscopic from this distance red dimension lights outlining the blocky body and long crane jib of a dragline. Once more, he got the strange impression that the workings were a domain of machines, devoid of human life. Perhaps it was just that the environment being created out there was so alien that it was impossible to imagine any life there.

Still, as he drifted away himself, he wondered drowsily if the men working the open cast ever slept.

He took a walk down into the town after breakfast to get some groceries. It was market day, and in the old marketplace bright awnings hung over ranks of stalls. He pottered amiably through the market, buying little things here and there for the house, before crossing the street into the covered shopping centre.

As a rule, he left shopping as long as possible and then bought enough to last until next time. He spent ten minutes in the grocer's, and came out with some groceries in an old cardboard box, leaving the rest to be delivered later in the day, and he walked home with the box under his arm.

On an impulse, he walked back along the old canal, and stood for a long time at the fence along the towpath, watching the machines hurrying mechanically about their business on the grey waste. Away down in the wide flat-bottomed valley was a great tumbled mire, where rain drained down off the hills and into the water table of the valley. Across the valley, directly parallel to but two hundred feet lower than the canal, the workings came up against a high railway embankment, which ran across the valley without a break and marked another boundary of the town. Beyond that there was another, lower embankment, and beyond that a mucky city-polluted river.

He looked back to the workings nearer at hand. In a drumming thunder of diesel, one of the great graders was making its way across the churned clay and mud; the windows of its cab were so coated with muck and mud that it was impossible to see its driver, which made the great machine look more and more like a great inhuman robot with a sentience of its own.

He frowned as the grader moved away, leaving in its wake a flat swathe of land its own width, as if it was laying behind itself some kind of road. Looking down at the graded path, his eye caught something small and pale poking up out of the churned clay at the edge, something like a thick stick. It struck him that it was the first sign of any trees he'd ever seen on the workings, and reminded him of the tree he'd worked on the day before. When the grader came back it would probably be buried again, and lost for ever.

Still frowning slightly, he put the box down in the grass beside one of the fenceposts, and very carefully climbed over the top strand of barbed wire and made his way down the slope on the other side. The clay was thick and sticky and clung in thick clods to his shoes and caked up his trouser bottoms as his feet sank into it.

The mud grew less firm at the bottom of the slope, and he went ankle-deep into it with every step, but the piece of stick beckoned him nevertheless, a little memory of life in this inhospitable place. He had to rescue it somehow.

He came across a patch of even more saturated ground, and he sank calf-deep into it with a sludgy squelching noise. He waded free, and then the stick was at his feet, yellow and smooth with the bark stripped off. He bent down and grasped it near the ground, and tugged it free of the clay. The clay gave it up reluctantly, with a barely audible sucking, and the moment he held it up in his hand he knew it wasn't a stick. It was far too heavy, and it was knobbed at both ends. He'd done research a year ago for a story he'd never been able to sell, so he knew what it was.

It was a man's thighbone.

Or a woman's, he reflected, back home in a clean pair of trousers and a Hawkwind teeshirt, nursing a mug of tea and staring at the bone on the sink draining board. By its length, he judged it to have come from someone around six feet tall, give or take six inches, and now it had been washed and all the impersonal muck scraped off, it seemed too white to have been in the ground long, though he had no way of telling how long. But it was definitely human in origin. He had no doubt of that.

What he ought to do now was telephone the local police and tell them about the bone. Chances were it belonged to some person who had gone missing from the town and had either had an accident on the site, or had been murdered for some reason and dumped there. The latter, it occurred to him, was more a product of his over-fertile imagination than anything else, but he didn't think it completely impossible.

However, it occurred to him that he had been trespassing on the site, and that even if the police did nothing to him, the company mining on the site would be sure to. He sipped his tea and pondered. In the living room the stereo was playing Rush's 'Xanadu', but he hardly heard it.

He could of course claim he had seen the bone and recognised it immediately for what it was, and then pretend that trespass had never occurred to him. He doubted that anyone would believe that he had gone after the bone thinking it was a stick, because he resented the mechanised hell out there on the hills and in the valley. Indeed, if he was honest with himself, the more he thought about it, the more flimsy the excuse seemed to him. It was probably better to leave well alone.

And then again, whoever the bone had belonged to, and however they had died, they would have had friends, relatives too, who didn't know what had become of the bone's owner. Didn't they deserve to know what had happened to him/her?

He drained his mug, and the tea was still hot enough to burn his throat. No. He was the only person who knew anything about it, and he'd always prided himself on having a strong but just conscience. Better to leave it than dredge up old pain for someone.

So, what then? Sitting there with the mug empty and cooling in his cupped hands, he found it difficult to imagine that pale smooth thing lying there in the bright sun as once having been clothed in flesh and blood and muscle, once part of a living, breathing, warm human being. It was just a length of bone, cold and dead, lying on the bright shining draining board. In its way, it was just as impersonal as the machines out there going coldly about their allotted tasks.

Now that he had made up his mind, there was nothing more he could do with the bone if he didn't tell the police. All he had done was save it from the machines. And in a way that was probably enough. A gesture against the steel and the diesel and the rubber and the waste. A last filial service to someone he could never have known.

The knock at the door made him start. He came up out of his reverie, suddenly aware of incidental things again. The mug was cold now; afternoon sunlight gushed aslant into the kitchen in bright rich stripes, falling on the table and across the smooth worn nub of the knee joint on the draining board. The stereo in the living room was silent, and there was a shape on the bubbled glass of the door, distorted by the bubbles.

The knock came again. He got up and walked to the door, leaving the mug on the table.

"Mr Bowman?"

He nodded. His father had Anglicised the family name before coming here in the early 'Fifties.

"Messages," said the man, proffering a cardboard box packed with boxes of cornflakes and soap powder. He was Scottish, with ginger hair and freckles.

He nodded, took the box, turned and put it on the table. When he turned back, the Scot had taken a bill from the back pocket of his cords and was holding it out with a felt tip pen. He took the bill, signed it, and handed bill and pen back.

"I haven't seen ye here before," the Scot remarked as he stuffed the slip of paper and the pen into his pocket.

He shook his head. "Been here about five months."

The Scot shook his head. "I wouldn't live here if ye paid me to," he said.

The wind was picking up again, making the wood outside the garden whisper and rustle, and on the wind came the deep thunder of the mining machines. The breeze disturbed the Scot's copper-bright hair.

"Wouldn't you?"

"I would not," said the Scot.

"Why not?"

"The last man who lived here, they found him dead in yon wee wood. Heart, so they say."

A frown deepened on his forehead. "Why should that make you afraid to live here?"

He put both hands in the back pockets of his cords and considered a moment before saying, "Ye ken, this is just what I heard later, but some folk do say, his face was all clawed and scratched, as if by some beast. But mind, that's just hearsay."

He stood there, caught suddenly by the extraordinarily vivid image. Nobody had told him anything about the house's previous owner; indeed, now he thought about it, the estate agent had been

150

oddly reticent about the subject. He had assumed that, whoever they had been, the previous owner had simply left for some reason or other. The possibility of their death had never occurred to him.

"Oh. How long ago was this?"

The Scot looked skyward a moment in thought. "It would be the year they began mining over the way. Three years."

"That's a long time ago. Three years is a long time to sell a house."

The Scot nodded. "I spoke to him the day before he died, and he seemed perfectly all right then. He was cutting wood."

He unconsciously rubbed his right shoulder, smiled when he realised what he was doing. "Cutting wood isn't all that easy."

The Scot smiled too. "Well, I'll bid you good day, sir."

He nodded. "Right. Thanks."

After the Scot had gone, he checked the box of groceries and put them away, then he washed out the mug and left it on the draining board, and stood for a moment before going into the living room. He turned over the Rush LP and put the stylus down, then turned on the electric typewriter and put a fresh sheet of paper into it, and as he put his fingers on the keys that vivid image came back to him, drumming with the phrase the Scot had used. '. . . all clawed and scratched, as if by some beast . . . some beast . . .'

 . . . *so Man prospered, built houses to protect himself from the night and the things living there, and he had light to drive the night back, and he began to cut down the forests, clearing the land to make way for cultivation, destroying the habitat of the old things, and one by one he began to forget them as they took on less and less importance in his life.*

And here we are today; most of the old forests are long gone and we're safe in our towns and cities, and we'd probably like to think that the old things have all gone, because they no longer belong to the world we've created. I think we're wrong.

The old things haven't gone; they're in hiding, some of them in the remnants of the old forests, some of them in the wild empty places where a few people go, some of them in the earth. Some of them have learned to adapt: they're living in the cities, in the sewers and alleyways, coming out at night, grubbing in dustbins for food. All of them waiting for us to make a slip, just biding their time until we're vulnerable or alone. We've despoiled their world, and when they do come out they're not going to be very nice about it . . .

He was sweating and tired, and the tips of his fingers ached because he had been hitting the keys far too hard. He sat back and closed his eyes, and in his mind marched great armies of elves in moonshone armour, slaughtering everything human, emptying the cities and leaving them to grow wild. And behind the elves marched the forests, returning to claim their lands.

He took a deep breath, let it out. Yes. Now he had something useful from all the thoughts he had been putting in order. A story of the last battle between men and the old things. And the moment the idea came to him, it seemed a weak insipid sort of consummation for the grand thoughts he had been having. Already it was becoming an adventure story. A little different from his usual style, but that was no bad thing, and if he worked on it, he might be able to elevate it from mere adventure story status. All he needed now was a short space of time in which to think before getting on with plotting out the story.

He hadn't meant to go back along the old canal, but after a while he ended up walking the towpath with the armies still marching in his head. He had been walking along the path for about a quarter of an hour before he consciously took stock of where he was.

He stopped and, standing quite still, listened to the sounds all around him. The machines dominated the world of sound, but very faint against them there was still the sound of birdsong. Sparrows, thrushes, the liquid, startled call of a blackbird in flight, all of them faint, but fighting against the tumbling thunder of the machines.

He looked across at the waste land on the other side of the fence, and wondered if the desolation was really as complete as it looked. After all, the entire area was meant to be landscaped when all the coal was gone. One day there would be grass, and trees on the hills, and lakes sparkling bright in the sun. The desolation was just a transient thing really. The wound would heal, grow new tissue.

There was something dark folded on the clay down below, partly buried, and folded in it a flash of orange. He stood for a long time looking at it before climbing over the fence and making his way down the slope again. He'd trespassed here once already, so he didn't think another time made much difference.

The dark thing was cloth of some kind. Heavy cloth, saturated with water and glistening on the mud. There seemed to be some kind of plastic too, orange. He bent down and pulled a corner of the cloth away, and the image sorted itself out. It was a donkey jacket, such as the workmen wore on the site. Probably lost or discarded. He gave it a tug to free it of the mud, and the orange plastic panel across the shoulders made a wet fluorescent flash in the colourless greyness. Beneath the cloth, something pale and yellow flashed dully. He noted that there were old treadmarks on the donkey jacket. More than two, as well, as if one of the machines had run over it repeatedly. He lifted the jacket to see what the pale flash had been, and stepped back with a gasp, his gorge rising as the stench hit him.

Half buried in the mud were the crushed splinters of a man's ribcage, and as he stepped away something fell from one of the sleeves of the jacket and slapped to the mud. It was broken and twisted, but he could make out radius and ulna and the elbow joint. A man's arm. He dropped the jacket and turned and ran.

It saved him.

The shock of finding the crushed skeleton had blocked out the awful noise of the huge grader, even as it bore blindly down on him. The few steps he ran only just carried him out of the great machine's path, and it thundered past him in a cloud of fumes just feet away, shaking the ground with its passage. His body reacted automatically, flinging him on his face in the stinking mud as the grader bounced past, spewing huge clay clods and spray from under its great filthy tyres.

He turned quickly as he hit the ground and watched the grader thunder away, his mind burning with the image of the dirty cab. The dirty cab whose door swung open, revealing that there was nobody driving the thing.

As he climbed trembling back up the bank, he realised that in trying to run him down, the grader had run over and buried the donkey jacket again.

The towpath came out about three hundred yards down the road from the main gate of the site. As he made his way wrathfully towards it a small group of people chanting slogans and carrying placards passed him going the other way on the opposite side of the road. For a moment he thought they might be conservationists protesting at the open casting, but when he read the placards he realised they were residents from a small village just outside the county border beyond the edge of the town. He remembered there had been some talk of the town absorbing the village, which would have meant revising the county border. The residents of the village were happy with the county they were in. The protesters passed him and went on up the road, their voices ringing clear and weak in the bright day. Futile.

The main gate was open, and he walked through it and up the road the lorries used to the tiny group of portable cabins which comprised the site offices.

A tall man wearing a donkey jacket and Wellingtons and carrying a hard hat was just coming out of one of the offices. "Can I help you?" The voice was amiable, but the eyes took in mud caked on cloth and flesh and grew suspicious.

"One of your machines almost killed me just now!" he exploded.

"I beg your pardon?"

He stopped, panting a little, shaking with reaction, then went on, "I saw a donkey jacket down on the workings when I was walking along the canal. When I went down to get it one of your graders almost ran over me. It was running away without a driver."

The other man's face grew hard. "If what you say is true, then you've been trespassing on private property," he said.

"Oh, for pity's sake, I was almost killed out there!"

The man in the donkey jacket frowned, then turned and went back into the office. Through the window, he could see the man examining a large pegboard on one wall of the cabin. He came out

154

a moment later and shook his head. "All our graders are occupied."

"Well one must have run away . . ." His voice trailed off. It was no good. "What do you do here?"

"Oh, I don't work here. I'm from Head Office. I've come to pick up some data on the landfills."

"How long have you been here?"

A shrug. A freshening breeze blew at his thinning hair. "A couple of hours."

"Is there anyone I can talk to who works here then?" Desperation blossomed.

The other shook his head. "Haven't seen anyone since I got here. They're all out on the site, I expect." He scowled. "Look, you shouldn't be here and I shouldn't be talking to you." He put a bundle of computer printout under his arm.

He nodded, suddenly feeling tired and a little sick. "Yes, all right. I'm going." And he walked away from the huts and back down the road to the main gate.

The house was sanctuary. He did subconscious things like shutting all the windows and putting a Black Sabbath album on the stereo and turning it up all the way. He sat down at the typewriter, then pushed the machine to one side and put his head on his arms on the table. He was shaking, and he felt very cold and tired with the realisation of what was really going on out at the workings. In his mind the armies of elves were already being replaced by drumming thundering ranks of filthy machines. The reason why the man at the site offices had seen no one was that there was no one to see any more. No one at all.

Because the machines had killed them all.

He sat up and rubbed his eyes. He didn't know what to do. Surely somebody ought to be told and the machines dealt with, but who was going to believe him? The man at the site had obviously accepted normality because the pegboard had implied it and because the computer which had given him his data was still running. Of course, a computer was just a machine too . . .

Still, somebody must have noticed that something was wrong,

surely. It depended, he supposed, on how long it had been going on. The crushed skeleton seemed to have been there for some time.

He sighed, and his eyes fell on the sheet of paper still caught in the typewriter. He automatically flipped through what he had written, but he kept getting caught on 'I think we're wrong . . . I think we're wrong . . . wrong . . .' It seemed to bring him out of it. A fiction; a dream.

Thinking rationally brought the impossibility of it to him. There were too many factors running against it. Machines didn't run themselves; they needed fuel, and presumably people to fuel them up, and to repair them. The dead workmen would be missed at once and something would be done about it.

No. He'd had a bad experience, and it had upset his reasoning for a short time, on top of all the thinking he had been doing beforehand about the return of the old things and the destruction of mankind. One train of thought had complemented the other.

He got up and went into the kitchen. Like a breeze blowing aside insubstantial billows of fog, the realisation of these factors displaced the nonsense he had been thinking.

He put the kettle on and made a pot of tea, his panacea for all ills, poured himself a big mugful, hotter and much stronger than he usually took it, and sat at the table sipping it. As he sat there he noticed the bone, still on the draining board. It struck him that the bone had contributed to the whole ridiculous train of thought in that bright afternoon. He got up from the table, leaving the mug steaming there, and took the bone by one end as he made his way to the door.

The wind had fallen now, and everything was still and silent, though he didn't notice the fact, or the absence of birdsong, as he strode down the garden, towards the stile and crossed through the hedge into the wilderness beyond the garden. He walked back along the hedge towards the wood, fully intending to chuck the wretched bit of bone away and try to forget it forever, but there was something wrong . . .

He stopped by the oak nearest the house, the bone hanging from his hand like a club, and tried to work out what was bothering him. Something about the wood was different; something had changed since yesterday. He leaned on the rough skin of the old oak and frowned, trying to deal with the sudden mental shift in direction. He had walked around the tree once, then once more, before it struck him what it was.

The wood wasn't different. It was the oak. It was nearer the wood than it had been the day before. There was a trail of churned earth about four yards long behind it, as if it had somehow moved away from the house since yesterday. The thing that had changed was the view of the wood from the oak now the oak had moved.

The wind suddenly came up as he stepped away from the tree, and the little wood murmured with it. It was almost as if the tree had moved away from the house because it associated the house with pain. He kept stepping away from the tree, unconsciously holding the bone as defence, until he was at the stile, and only then did he turn his back on the tree and flee for the sanctuary of the house.

With all the windows shut, the doors locked, curtains drawn and the stereo blasting out 'Megalomania' at full volume, he could still hear the wind howl and cry in the wood like something being tortured, and its voice in the trees was terribly, terribly old.

He sat cross-legged in front of the roaring fire, staring fixedly into the flames, bathed in radiant heat, but deep inside he felt a bright knot of cold growing, feeding upon itself. Outside, night was growing on the world like a great malevolent shadow. He could hear, faint but very deep, just fighting its way through the thick curtains, the noise of the great machines on the workings. Inside him, the cold presence shivered.

He had to be wrong, mistaken. He couldn't possibly be right, but he was too scared to go back outside and make sure. If the oak had moved, then the thought of the machines on the workings working themselves of their own volition was no longer so unlikely. If the tree had moved, then everything he had thought of today was equally possible, even against all the attendant impossibilities.

If it was all actually happening, what then were the machines doing? Adapting the world to their own liking, perhaps? Making their own bid for ascendancy, as Man had done all those thousands of years ago, when he began to clear the forests?

There was a scratching sound on the wall, and he looked up, confused and suddenly disorientated. The scratching came again, and with it a soft rustling sound from outside. The Black Sabbath track ended, and the tracking arm came up with a soft thump, moved back to the rest, clicked, came down on the rest, and with another click the unit turned itself off. The speakers hissed subliminally, then the rustling noises came back. This time they seemed all around him.

He got up and went to the window and half-heartedly pulled one of the curtains back, and he stood there frozen by the thing he saw.

Standing outside in the garden were tall, arthritic shapes with gnarled, twisted heads; six of them standing there in the early moonlight. He could see where they had broken through the hedge, and the churned earth of the flowerbeds which marked their passage onto the ripped lawn. The wind cried in their foliage, and it suddenly struck him that he had made the mistake of anthropomorphising the old things. There were no elves in moonshone armour; the trees were the oldest things on the earth.

He dropped the curtain and ran upstairs and stood at the bedroom window looking down at the trees. He couldn't see them moving; either they were simply standing there waiting, or they moved too slowly to gauge.

A quick check at all the upstairs windows confirmed his fears. The trees were all around the house, a ragged ring two or three deep and without break.

The quote from Macbeth about the Wood of Birnam came bursting back to him, and he wondered if Shakespeare could possibly have known. It raged its way up from his memories of O-level English, and with it hard, cold, vivid memories of his earlier schooldays, which had been agony after the other kids had discovered his father was German. The images flipped across him, faded to allow another to resolve. He'd once seen a rock in the Lake District, split in two by the roots of a tree. A huge rock, almost fifteen feet high, and the tree had split it like a hazelnut.

He took a long deep breath and held it a moment, his whole body stiffened, while all the images sorted themselves out, and when he exhaled again he was calm and reasoning once more and he had formulated a plan to save his life. Something wild and drastic, but tailored by and for the situation, and he knew its shape and form precisely.

The gallon polythene jerry of paraffin was still in the cupboard under the sink. It was still three-quarters full, and the liquid inside slopped about as he carried it back upstairs. He unscrewed the cap and slung great pungent swathes of the paraffin in all the upstairs rooms, soaking the bed and furniture. He took sheets out of the airing cupboard, twisting and soaking them and making great long fuses of them, leading out of each room to join a single length of sheets in the landing. He laid this down the stairs, soaking it as he went, and down into the hall, where he ran out of paraffin. The other jerry under the sink was full, and he carried it calmly from the cupboard, keeping to the shape of his plan.

He made piles of paraffin-soaked cloth in the living room and kitchen, then he stood a moment considering before taking the Sabbath record off the stereo. He took his old dear copy of Deep Purple's 'Burn' out of the rack and put it on the turntable, activated the autochange. As the arm came over and down, he took his sheets of typed notes and twisted them into a torch and put the end into the fire. They caught instantly, a slow steady flame, and he turned and touched them to the paraffin-wet pile of cloth, which burst into light and sound and heat. He did the same in the hall, touching the fuse cloth. The flame leapt up it with a greedy roar and up onto the landing, dividing, and into each of the upstairs rooms, and he heard the things there ignite. The brand was burning close to his hand now. He ran through the kitchen, opened the door, turned a moment in the gust of cold air, and tossed the brand at the sodden heap in the middle of the kitchen floor, then turned and ran as it took hold.

The trees were crying in the wind. Perhaps they knew what he had done. Perhaps they could not move away quickly enough to escape the fire. From inside the house came a low powerful roaring. He put his head down and ran at the screen of trees.

Branches and twigs ripped at his face and hair, scratching and tearing him (all clawed and scratched, as if by some beast . . .) and then he was through, bruised and bleeding, but still alive and on his feet. He turned right and jumped the hedge. Something snagged his ankle, and he went down heavily on the other side, rolled up, felt his trousers tear, and ran on across the field.

As he reached the high-hedged lane which led down to the town, something exploded in the house; the gas main perhaps, but all he felt was a fading sense of loss for all his destroyed possessions. He'd outsmarted the old things. Out on the open cast, the new things thundered. Battle was declared. Everything encroaches. It wasn't his battle, though; he'd won his battle, and his laugh rang in the clear air as he ran down between the hedges towards the bright, beckoning town, and it might have been his imagination, but the hedges seemed to be leaning closer together in order to hear his triumphant laughter . . .